FORMS OF DEVOTION

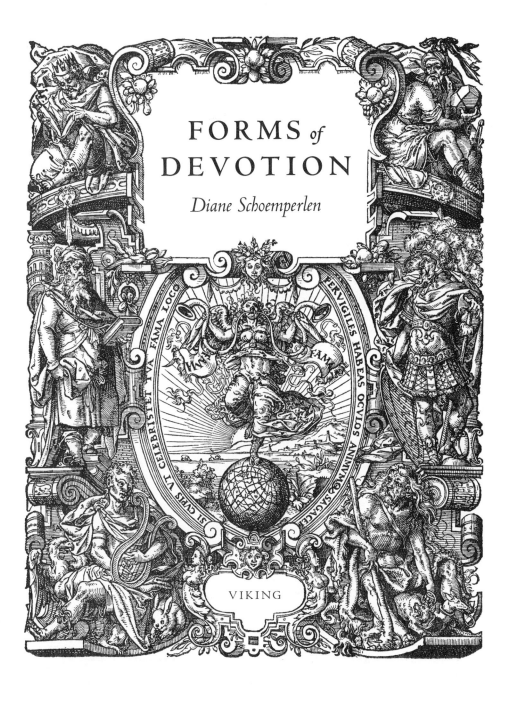

FORMS of DEVOTION

Diane Schoemperlen

VIKING

c,)

VIKING
Published by the Penguin Group
Penguin Putnam Inc., 375 Hudson Street, New York, New York 10014, U.S.A.
Penguin Books Ltd, 27 Wrights Lane, London W8 5TZ, England
Penguin Books Australia Ltd, Ringwood, Victoria, Australia
Penguin Books Canada Ltd, 10 Alcorn Avenue, Toronto, Ontario, Canada M4V 3B2
Penguin Books (N.Z.) Ltd, 182–190 Wairau Road, Auckland 10, New Zealand

Penguin Books Ltd, Registered Offices: Harmondsworth, Middlesex, England

First published in 1998 by Viking Penguin,
a member of Penguin Putnam Inc.

1 3 5 7 9 10 8 6 4 2

The following stories have been previously published in slightly different form: "Forms of Devotion" appeared in *Saturday Night* (Toronto, April 1996); "The Spacious Chambers of Her Heart" in *Border/Lines* (Toronto, no. 28, 1993) and *Story* (Cincinnati, Autumn 1996); and "Body Language" in *Exile* (Toronto, vol. 18, no. 2, 1994) and *Story* (Cincinnati, Spring 1997).

Excerpt from "The Love Song of J. Alfred Prufrock" from *Collected Poems 1909–1962* by T. S. Eliot, published by Harcourt Brace & Company and Faber and Faber Ltd.

Publisher's Note
These selections are works of fiction. Names, characters, places, and incidents either are the product of the author's imagination or are used fictitiously, and any resemblance to actual persons, living or dead, events, or locales is entirely coincidental.

LIBRARY OF CONGRESS CATALOGING IN PUBLICATION DATA
Schoemperlen, Diane.
Forms of devotion / Diane Schoemperlen.
p. cm.
ISBN 0-670-87696-8
I. Title.
PR9199.3.S267F6   1998
813'.54—dc21   97-24278

This book is printed on acid-free paper.

Printed in the United States of America
Set in Centaur
Designed by Francesca Belanger

For my son, Alexander,
who said it was too bad my books
didn't have pictures in them

CONTENTS

FORMS OF
DEVOTION

Strangely enough we are all seeking a form of devotion which fits our sense of wonder. —J. Marks, *Transition*

I. FAITH

The faithful are everywhere. They climb into their cars each morning and drive undaunted into the day. They sail off to work, perfectly confident that they will indeed get there: on time, intact. It does not occur to them that they could just as well be broadsided by a Coca-Cola delivery truck running the red light at the corner of Johnson and Main. They do not imagine the bottles exploding, the windshield shattering, their chests collapsing, the blood spurting out of their ears. They just drive. The same route every day, stop and go, back and

forth, and yes, they get there: safe and sound. In the same unremarkable manner, they get home again too. Then they start supper without ever once marveling at the fact that they have survived. It does not occur to them that the can of tuna they are using in the casserole might be tainted and they could all be dead of botulism by midnight.

They are armed with faith. They trust, if not in God exactly, then in the steadfast notion of everyday life. They do not expect to live forever of course, but they would not be entirely surprised if they did. On a daily basis, death strikes them mostly as a calamity which befalls other people, people who are probably evil, careless, or unlucky: just in the wrong place at the wrong time.

On weekend mornings, the faithful take their children to the park and assume they will not be abducted or fondled behind the climber by a pervert in a trench coat. In the afternoons, they work in their gardens, quite confident that those tiny seeds will eventually produce more tomatoes, zucchini, and green beans than they will know what to do with. They dig in the dirt and believe in the future. They put up preserves, save for retirement, and look forward to being grandparents. After they retire, they plan to buy a motor home and travel.

When they go to bed at night, they assume that their white houses will stay standing, their green gardens will keep growing, their pink babies will keep breathing, and the yellow sun will rise in the morning just as it always does. Many of the faithful are women, giving birth being, after all, the ultimate act of pure faith. When their sons and daughters (whose as yet embryonic faith may temporarily fail them) wake sobbing from nightmares and wail, "Mommy, I dreamed you were dead. You won't die, will you?" these faithful mothers say, in all honesty, "Don't worry, I won't." The faithful sleep soundly.

If ever they find themselves feeling unhappy or afraid (as sometimes they do because, although faithful, they are also still human), they assume this too shall pass. They expect to be safe. They expect to be saved in the long run. They are devoted to the discharge of their daily lives. It does not occur to them that the meaning of life may be open to question.

II. MEMORY

MEMORIA.

Remember to put out the garbage, pick up the dry cleaning, defrost the pork chops (the ground beef, the chicken thighs, the fillet of sole). Remember to feed the dog (the cat, the hamster, the goldfish, the canary). Remember the first smile, the first step, the first crush, the first kiss. Remember the bright morning, the long hot afternoon, the quiet evening, the soft bed, gentle rain in the night. Also remember the pain, the disappointments, the humiliations, the broken hearts, and an eclectic assortment of other sorrows. Take these tragedies in stride and with dignity. Do not tear your hair out. Forgive and forget and get on with it. The faithful look back fondly.

They are only passingly familiar with shame, guilt, torment, chaos, existentialism, and metaphysics. The consciences of the faithful are clear. They are not the ones spending millions of dollars on self-help books and exercise videos. They know they've done the best they could. If and when the faithful make mistakes, they know how to forgive themselves without requiring years of expensive therapy in the process.

In the summer, remember the winter: snow sparkling in clear sunlight, children in puffy snowsuits building snowmen and sucking icicles. Remember hockey rinks, rosy cheeks, Christmas carols, wool socks, and hot chocolate with marshmallows. In the winter, remember the summer: tidy green grass beneath big blue sky, long-limbed children playing hide-and-go-seek and running through sprinklers. Remember barbecues, sailboats, flowers, strawberries, and pink lemonade. The faithful can always find something to look forward to. The faithful never confuse the future with the past.

III. KNOWLEDGE

The knowledge of the faithful is vast. They know how to change a tire on a deserted highway in the middle of the night without getting dirty or killed. They know how to bake a birthday cake in the shape of a bunny rabbit with gumdrop eyes and a pink peppermint nose. They know how to unplug a clogged drain with baking soda and vinegar.

They know how to paint the hallway, refinish the hardwood floors, wallpaper the bedroom, insulate the attic, reshingle the roof, and install a new toilet. They know how to build a campfire and pitch a tent single-handedly. They know how to tune up the car, repair the furnace, and seal the storm windows to prevent those nasty and expensive winter drafts.

They know how to prepare dinner for eight in an hour and a half for less than twenty dollars. They know how to sew, knit, crochet, and cut hair. They know how to keep themselves, their houses, their cars, and their children clean, very clean. They do not resent having to perform the domestic duties of family life. They may even enjoy doing the laundry, washing the walls, cleaning the oven, and grocery shopping. They know how to make love to the same person for twenty years without either of them getting bored. They know how to administer CPR and the Heimlich maneuver. They know how and when to have fun.

The faithful know exactly what to say at funerals, weddings, and cocktail parties. They know when to laugh and when to cry and they never get these two expressions of emotion mixed up. The faithful know they are normal and they're damn proud of it. What they don't know won't hurt them.

IV. INNOCENCE

INOCENTIA.
A Magis illuditur Herodes. Eis iratus omnes
pueros a bimulis et infra curat interficiendos.

Die Unschuld.
Der Unschuldig Kinder Orden
läßt Herodes grausam morden.

The faithful are so innocent. Despite all evidence to the contrary, they believe that deep down everybody is just like them, or could be. They believe in benevolence, their own and other people's. They think that, given half a chance, even hardened criminals and manic-depressives can change. They are willing to give everyone a second chance. For the faithful, shaking off doubt is as easy as shaking a rug.

The faithful believe in law and order. They still look up to policemen, lawyers, teachers, doctors, and priests. They believe every word these people say. They even believe what the radio weatherman says in the forecast right after the morning news. It does not occur to them that these authority figures could be wrong, corrupt, or just plain stupid. Mind you, even the faithful are beginning to have serious reservations about politicians.

The faithful take many miraculous things for granted. Things like skin, electricity, trees, water, fidelity, the dogged revolution of the earth around the sun. They believe in beauty as a birthright and surround themselves with it whenever they can. They believe in interior decorating and makeup. They never underestimate the degree of happiness to be engendered by renovating the kitchen, placing fresh-cut flowers on the table, purchasing a set of fine silver, a mink coat, a minivan, or miscellaneous precious jewels. The faithful still believe you get what you pay for.

The faithful take things at face value. They do not search for hidden meanings or agendas. They are not skeptical, cynical, or suspicious. They are not often ironic. The faithful are the angels among us.

V. STRENGTH

The faithless say the faithful are fools. Obviously it must be getting more and more difficult to keep the faith these days. Read the paper. Watch the news. Wonder what the world is coming to. All things considered, it has become harder to believe than to despair.

The faithless say the faithful are missing the point. But secretly the faithless must admit that if indeed, as they allege, there is no point (no purpose, no reason, no hope), then the faithful aren't missing a thing.

The faithless say the faithful are living minor lives, trivial, mundane, frivolous, blind. But secretly the faithless must envy the faithful, wondering if they themselves are simply too fainthearted for faith.

While the faithless gaze into the abyss, fretting, moaning, and brooding, the faithful are busy getting on with their lives: laboring, rejoicing, carving Halloween pumpkins, roasting Christmas and Thanksgiving turkeys, blowing out birthday candles year after year, and kissing each other wetly at midnight on New Year's Eve.

No matter what, the faithful know how to persevere. They are masters of the rituals that protect them. To the faithful, despair is a foreign language which they have neither the time nor the inclination to learn. The faithful frequently sing in the shower.

The faithful understand the value of fortitude. They carry always with them the courage of their convictions. They do not go to extremes but they could perform miracles if they had to. The faithful will not be crushed by the weight of the world. The faithful are sturdy and brave.

VI. IMAGINATION

The faithful have their imaginations well in hand. They do not lie awake at night imagining earthquakes, tornadoes, flash floods, or nuclear war. They do not deal in cataclysms. They do not entertain the possibility of being axed to death in their beds by a psychokiller on the loose from the psychiatric hospital on the eastern edge of town. They do not lie there wide-eyed for hours picturing malignant cells galloping through their uteruses, their intestines, their prostate glands, or their brains. To the faithful, a headache is a headache, not a brain tumor. They do not imagine themselves rotting away from the inside out. They do not have detailed sexual fantasies about the mailman, the aerobics instructor, or their children's Grade Two teacher. The nights of the faithful are peaceful. Even their nightmares have happy endings. The faithful wake up smiling. Their subconsciouses are clear.

Imagine perfect health, financial security, your mortgage paid off, a new car every second year. Imagine mowing the lawn on Sunday afternoon and enjoying it. Imagine raking leaves in the fall without having to contemplate the futility of daily life. Imagine your grandchildren sitting at your knee while you tell them the story of your life.

The faithful are seldom haunted by a pesky sense of impending doom. They imagine that their lives are unfolding as they were meant to. They imagine that they are free. They imagine finding their feet planted squarely on the road to heaven. The faithful are prepared to live happily ever after.

Imagine laughing in the face of the future.

Imagine belonging to the fine fierce tribe of the faithful.

VII. PRAYER

Pray for sunshine, pray for rain. Pray for peace. Pray for an end to the suffering of the unfortunate. Pray silently in a language simple enough for a child to understand. It is not necessary to get down on your knees with your eyes closed, your hands clasped. It is not necessary to hold your breath. Pray while you are cooking dinner, doing the dishes, washing the floor, holding your sleeping child in your arms. Pray with your heart, not just your mouth.

The faithful know how to pray to whatever gods they may worship. The faithful are praying all the time, every step of the way. Their prayers are not the sort that begin with the word *Please.* They do not bargain with their gods for personal favors. They do not make promises they can't keep, to their gods or anyone else. They do not beg for money, power, easy answers, or a yellow Porsche. They do not beseech, petition, implore, solicit, entreat, adjure, or snivel. They do not throw themselves upon the unreliable mercy of the pantheon. They are not dramatic zealots. The faithful are dignified, stalwart, and patient. All things come to them who will but wait. They are committed to simply enduring in a perpetual state of grace. Their faith itself is a never-ending benediction. The faithful may or may not go to church on Sunday. Their faith is their business.

The prayers of the faithful are mostly wordless forms of devotion. Actions speak louder than language. The faithful are reverent, humble, blessed. They are always busy having a religious experience. The faithful are seldom alarmed or afraid. The faithful barely have time to notice that all their prayers have been answered.

VIII. ABUNDANCE

ABUNDANTIA.
Deficient tandem magni patrimonia Croesi,
Verum, quod Solon vaticinatur, erat.

Der Überfluß.
Croefi Reichthum fan sich enden
Und was Solon sagt, einfinden.

The faithful have more than enough of everything. They are never stingy. They believe in abundance and they know how to share the wealth. They give regularly to local and international charities and to most panhandlers. They give their old clothes and toys to the poor. The faithful are always generous. Of course they can afford to be. Of course there's more where that came from.

Every evening at dinner the faithful cry, "More, more, let's have some more!" The table is completely covered with heavy oval platters of meat and giant bowls of mashed potatoes and garden salad. They always have dessert. They prefer their children soft and plump. The faithful never bite off more than they can chew.

The days of the faithful are as full as their stomachs. They have energy to burn. They never whine about having too much to do. They like to be busy. They do not need time to think. Their bounty abounds. Their homes and their hearts are always full. Full of exuberance or solemnity, whichever current circumstances may require. The cups of the faithful frequently runneth over.

The arms of the faithful are always open. They have time for everyone. The faithful know how to share both the triumphs and the sorrows of others. They've always got the coffee on, blueberry muffins in the oven, a box of Kleenex handy just in case. The faithful know how to listen and they only offer advice when they're asked.

The faithful know how to count their blessings, even if it takes all day. They have all the time in the world. They know when to thank their lucky stars. The faithful are privileged but they are not smug.

IX. WISDOM

The faithful are uncommonly wise. They are indefatigably glad to be alive. To the faithful everything matters. It does not occur to them that their whole lives may well end up having been nothing but a waste of time. The faithful are always paying attention. They know how to revel in the remarkable treasures of the everyday: a pink rose blooming below the window, a ham and cheese omelet steaming on the plate, a white cat washing her face in the sun, a new baby with eyes the color of sand, a double rainbow in the western sky after a long hard rain.

The faithful love rainbows and pots of gold. They know how to take pleasure wherever they can find it. The faithful are always exclaiming, "Look, look, look at that!" To the faithful nothing is mundane.

The faithful are everywhere. See if you can spot them: in the bank lineup on Friday afternoon, at McDonald's having hamburgers and chocolate milkshakes with their children, in the park walking the dog at seven o'clock on a January morning, at the hardware store shopping for a socket wrench and a rake. The faithful may be right in your own backyard.

The faithful are thankful for small pleasures and small mercies.

The faithful are earnest.

The faithful are easily amused.

The faithful do or do not know how lucky they are.

The faithful frequently cry at parades.

The faithful are not afraid of the dark because they have seen the light.

Nothing is lost on the faithful. As far as they are concerned, wonders will never cease. The faithful are convinced that the best is yet to come.

X. HOPE

SPES.

Palæstina, quam Deus Abraam, Isaac et Iacob promiserat,
ostenditur Mosi, habitatio vero in illa ei non conceditur.
Mortuum sepelivit Deus: Sepulturæ locus adhuc incertus est.

Die Hofnung.
Moses soll das Land zwar sehen,
aber nicht hinüber gehen.

The hope of the faithful is a tonic.
Their eyes are bright, their skin is
clear, their hair is shiny, and their
blood flows vigorously through all
of their veins. Even in times of ad-
versity, the faithful know how to
take heart. At the tiniest tingle of
possibility, the faithful are not
afraid to get their hopes up. They
believe in divine providence. It all
depends on how you define *divine.*
The faithful are not fools. Although
the faithless would dispute this, the
faithful live in the real world just as
much as anyone. They know all
about hoping against hope. But they
are not troubled by paradox. They are immune to those fits of despair
which can cripple and dumbfound.

Concerning matters both big and small, the faithful have always
got hope. Their whole lives are forms of perpetual devotion to the
promise which hope extends. The faithful breathe hope like air, drink
it like water, eat it like popcorn. Once they start, they can't stop.

Hope for world peace. Hope for a drop in the crime rate, shelter
for the homeless, food for the hungry, rehabilitation for the deranged.
Hope your son does well on his spelling test. Hope your team wins

the World Series. Hope your mother does not have cancer. Hope the pork chops are not undercooked. Hope your best friend's husband is not having an affair with his secretary. Hope you win the lottery. Hope the rain stops tomorrow. Hope this story has a happy ending.

The hope of the faithful is infinite, ever expanding to fill the space available. Faith begets hope. Hope begets faith. Faith and hope beget power.

The faithful lean steadily into the wind.

FIVE
SMALL ROOMS
(A MURDER MYSTERY)

I have learned not to underestimate the power of rooms, especially a small room with unequivocal corners, exemplary walls, and well-mannered windows divided into many rectangular panes. I like a small room without curtains, carpets, misgivings, or ghosts.

I. SMALL ROOM WITH PEARS

I like a room painted in a confident full-bodied color. I steer clear of pastels because they are, generally speaking, capricious, irresolute, and frequently coy. Blue is a good color for a small room, especially if it is of a shade called Tidal Pool, Tropical Sea, Azure, Atoll, or Night Swim.

I once painted a room a shade of blue called Rainy Day. I find a rainy day to be a fine thing on occasion, particularly after an unmitigated stretch of gratuitous sunshine. In that blue room, I kept a stock

of umbrellas ready at hand just in case. This was the first room I had ever painted all by myself. For years I had believed that painting a room was a task I could never master, a task better left to professionals or men. After I finished painting this room, I was as proud of myself as if I had discovered the Northwest Passage.

This room had many outstanding features including lots of large cupboards and a counter ample enough to perform surgery on if necessary. In the cupboards I kept all kinds of things: dresses that no longer fit or flattered me, a bird's nest I'd found in the park when I was six, a red and white lace negligee, the program from a musical version of *Macbeth*, several single socks and earrings, instruction manuals for a radio, a blow-dryer, and a lawn mower that I no longer owned, a package of love letters tied up with a black satin ribbon. No matter how many secrets I stowed in these cupboards, they never filled up.

Often I found myself wandering into the blue room in the middle of the night. I would stand naked staring into the refrigerator at three in the morning, until the cold air gave me goose bumps and my nipples got hard. It was a very old refrigerator which sometimes chirped like a distant melancholy cricket. I was searching not for food so much as for memories, motives, an alibi: how it looked, how it happened, when.

I would reach into the refrigerator and pull out a chunk of ham, a chicken leg, a slice of cheese, or some fruit. Pears were my favorite. Imagine the feel of the sweet gritty flesh on your tongue, the voluptuous juice on your chin. Pears are so delicate. My fingertips made bruises on their thin mottled skin.

This was nothing like "The Love Song of J. Alfred Prufrock": *Shall I part my hair behind? Do I dare to eat a peach? / I shall wear white flannel trousers, and walk upon the beach. / I have heard the mermaids singing, each to each.* Peaches I am not fond of. Their fuzz gives me shivers like fingernails on a chalkboard. The color of their flesh close to the pit is too much like that of meat close to the bone. My consumption of pears had nothing to do with daring or indecision. It was strictly a matter of pure pleasure, which always comes as a great relief. At that point in my life I'd had no dealings with mermaids and did not expect to. I am tone deaf and, much as I admire a good body of water, I have never learned to swim.

As for the women who come and go, they are not likely to be talking of Michelangelo.

II. SMALL ROOM WITH SEASHELLS

Later there was another small blue room, this one painted in a shade called Atlantis because it was situated on the very edge of the ocean. In this room I enjoyed the omnipresent odor of salt water and the ubiquitous sound of the surf. These struck me as two things I would never grow tired of.

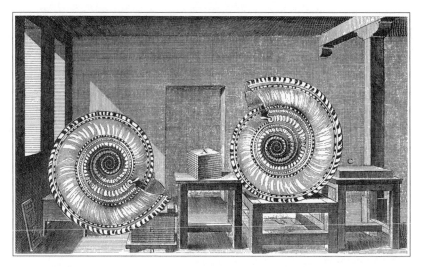

This room was very sturdy, with support beams as substantial and steadfast as tree trunks. The windows were recessed deep into the thick outer walls. These walls were solid straight through, not hollow in the middle like most. They put me in mind of chocolate Easter bunnies, how the best bunnies are the solid ones, how cheated you feel when biting into a hollow one only to discover it is just a thin shell of chocolate around a rabbit-shaped pocket of sweet empty air.

Here I often wandered out to the beach in the middle of the night. I did not wear white flannel trousers and I never heard the mermaids singing. I had no desire to disturb the universe. I simply stood there with my toes in the ocean and my head in the sky. The hair on my arms stood up in the moonlight. I studied the constellations and thought about words like *firmament, nebula,* and *galactic cannibalism.* I had to keep reminding myself that some of the stars I was seeing were already dead. I had trouble at first with the whole notion of light-years, with time as a function of distance, speed, and illumination, rather than as simply the conduit from then to now.

On cloudy nights, when I could not pursue the perfection of my theory of stars, I turned instead to collecting the miscellaneous offerings which the ocean so munificently deposited at my feet.

I gathered seashells by the fistful, listened for the ocean in each of them, and it was always there, like the same moon seen from every continent, the same God petitioned in every prayer. From the sand I plucked moon shells, harp shells, angel wings, helmets, goblets, butterflies, cockles, and tusks. Less plentiful and so of course more desirable were the sundial and chambered nautilus shells. I'd read somewhere once how the young cephalopod at first lives in the center of its shell but as it grows larger, it must move forward, sealing off each chamber behind itself. This would be like shutting a door and having it permanently locked behind you.

The seashells, like the stars, were long dead, the beautiful cast-off husks of the ugly mollusks that had made them. Only these pretty skeletons had survived, just as it was only the light of the stars that could still reach me. I thought long and hard about chambers, skeletons, a series of small rooms, the missing bodies of seashells and stars.

There were other things too offered up by the sea: tangled balls of fishing line, plastic bags, a bracelet, a knife. A pair of panty hose, a set of keys, a bathing suit, and several used condoms. Pieces of driftwood like bones, coils of seaweed like entrails. One night I found a water-bloated copy of a murder mystery called *Dead Dead Double Dead.* The last five pages were missing. This, I could not help but think, was hitting a little too close to home.

Apparently the ocean, in addition to being a weighty and ambivalent symbol of dynamic forces, transitional states, the collective unconscious, chaos, creation, and universal womanhood in all its benevolent and heinous incarnations, was also the repository of all lost things. I had long wondered what happened to those socks that went into the washing machine and never came out.

At this time I still believed that I could summon up my former self whenever I was ready, that I could gather up my innocence and step back into it like an old pair of shoes. Now I began to see this was no longer true. Eventually I realized that in this small room I was forever in danger of drowning or being swallowed by a sea monster. This epiphany marked the end of my blue period.

III. SMALL ROOM WITH CATS

Various shades of brown are good for small rooms too. Brown imparts a sense of serenity, solidity, and security. Imagine lying down on a bed of warm soil. Imagine being buried alive and liking it. I am partial to any color of brown that looks like coffee with milk in it or any shade that is named after food: Honey Nut, Bran Muffin, Caramel Chip, or Indian Corn. In a small room painted a color called Pumpkin Loaf, I always felt full. Sometimes in the morning I thought I could smell the sweet bread baking.

In this room there were tables but no chairs. Clearly the importance of chairs has been overestimated. I quickly got over my atavistic longings for them. Soon enough I could hardly imagine what I'd ever deemed to be indispensable about chairs. Like so many other things I once thought I could never live without, chairs, once I got used to their absence, proved to be just another habit, a knee-jerk reflex like flinching, apologizing, or falling in love. The only time I seriously missed them was when I wanted to sit down and tie my shoes. This was like wishing for a man when you want to clean out the eavestrough or open a new jar of pickles.

There were also many shelves in this brown room, tidy well-spaced shelves like boxes built right into the wall. Some of them still bore items left behind by some former fugitive tenant. There was a pink lampshade which, in a happier time, I might have put on my head. There were some pale yellow bed sheets, soft from many washings, stained with the bodily fluids of long-gone strangers. No matter where you go, you are always leaving incriminating tidbits of evidence behind you.

There was a stack of old *National Geographic* magazines. Everyone has a pile of these stashed away somewhere. There were also several empty picture frames propped up on the shelves and hammered to the walls. I carefully cut photographs from the magazines and stuck them in these frames. I selected several panoramic views of jungles, mountains, fields of wheat. I chose skies without clouds, seas without boats, landscapes without figures. I changed these pictures often so as not to feel that I was just treading water or running in place.

Here I kept cats for company. I like the look of a small room with two cats in it. I tried to emulate the way they can settle themselves anywhere like boneless shape-shifting pillows and how, when falling from a great height, they will almost always land on their feet. I was impressed too by their apparently infinite ability to adapt, the way they can live well anywhere: in an alley, a barn, a palace, or a small brown room with tables and shelves, no chairs.

I told my cats stories of other cats, famous cats, tenacious cats, heroic cats, miraculous cats who found their way home again after traveling through endless miles of wilderness, fording rivers, scaling canyons, leaping tall buildings with a single bound. My cats curled around me and purred. It is not true that cats only purr when they're happy. They also do it when they're worried or in pain.

In my time I have been accused of many things: jealousy, arrogance, selfishness, viciousness, laziness, bitterness, and lust. Also infidelity, inclemency, insanity, immorality, and pride. I have been called reckless, heartless, shameless, malicious, sarcastic, demanding, domineering, cold-blooded, and cruel. The cats, of course, knew none of this and did not care to ask. They were well aware of the perils of curiosity, the trials and tribulations of being misunderstood. There is always someone who will be offended by a cat's enthusiasm for killing. Think of the way they play with their prey and then, once it is sufficiently dead, how they always eat the head first, often swallowing it whole. Think of the way they leave the hearts behind, those slimy little lumps drawing flies in the driveway. Myself, I do not find this distasteful. There is always someone who will tell you that your instincts are wrong. Outside, the sweet yellow fog pressed against the windowpanes.

IV. SMALL ROOM WITH MOTH

Most kinds of green paint, as you would expect, are named after pastoral scenes and growing things: Meadow, Pasture, Orchard, Leaf, Broccoli, Asparagus, Spinach, and Dill. In a small room painted a shade called Forest Lane, the air was always moist, emitting an intimate odor of new growth and decay. The light was leafy and diffuse, like a green glaze on my skin. The ceiling was done in Maiden of the Mist, a humid color much like that of the sky on a hazy August afternoon. If I stared at this ceiling for too long, I found I could not catch my breath.

Where the walls met the ceiling there were curves instead of straight lines and angles. The tops of the windows and doorway were vaulted too. I enjoyed these arches the way you enjoy a symphony, your whole body thrilling at the crescendo's inevitable approach. I like a good old-fashioned symphony, the way it stirs the blood. At this point in my life I knew I was ripe for a transformation.

In this room there were many solid wooden benches, the purpose of which was never clear. Perhaps the room had once been the meeting place of a secret cult whose members would sit on these benches in rows of black cloaks and hoods, worshiping their various devils and

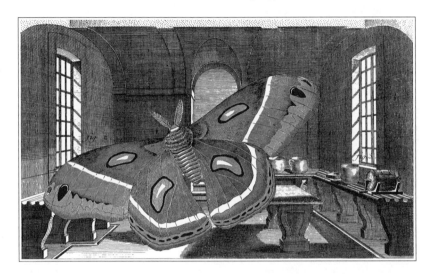

gods, planning their next move. Arranged upon these mysterious benches was an impressive assortment of cookware, metal pots and bowls of many sizes, some battered, some smooth. Perhaps these had been used to boil the sacrificial virgins or lambs. My desires both to cook and to eat having been dislodged by the heat and my overactive imagination, I filled these vessels with flowers instead of stew, sacrificial or otherwise. In this green room I ate only raw green things: lettuce, celery, sweet peppers, and limes.

Here I did not wander at night. I still went to bed not knowing what I had been accused of but this uncertainty no longer tormented me. I had only two bad dreams during my sojourn in this green room. The first was of having my head shriveled to the size of a small sweet pepper, then sliced in half and served upon a big green platter. The second was of having my body covered with a fine white powder and then pinned still wriggling to the wall. It was not a green wall. It was a red wall. I slept flat on my back with the windows open and a candle burning on the floor beside me.

Moths flew in through the open windows, misguided emissaries from the unbridled night. The patterns on their wings were written in a language I did not yet understand. They came from miles around, unable to resist the sweet deadly pull of the flame any more than I could ever resist a ripe pear, a good murder mystery, or a man who said he could save me. Moths, like humans, engage in complicated court-ship rituals which involve elaborate dances and sudden dazzling flights. It was hard to determine whether they were courting each other or the promise of a hot dramatic death. I could have reached up from my bed and touched them. But as a child I was told you must never touch a moth because if that fine powder is rubbed off its wings, it will die. Outside, I thought I heard voices but I was mistaken.

I did not touch the moths. They died anyway. In the morning I would find their corpses littering the floor around my guttered candle. Their beautiful wings were scorched, their feathery antennae fried, that magic powder turned to ash. There was a lesson to be learned here, something about fortitude and the purification of the soul by fire. Either that or the moths were simply too stupid to survive. Some people believe that white moths are actually the souls of the dead and that if a black moth flies into a house, it means that someone who lives there will die within the year.

Looking back on my own life, it is hard to determine which was the moth and which was the flame. In these matters, there is no such thing as black and white.

V. SMALL ROOM WITH CLOCKS

I have learned to be wary of the purples which have names like Dazzle, Delusion, Charade, Mirage, and Masquerade. When I first painted this small room a shade of purple called New Year's Eve, it was easy to fool myself into believing that here I could make time stand still. I imagined myself poised in the middle of the countdown to midnight. All around me expectant voices chanted: *Ten nine eight seven six five.* Then they stopped. Thousands of upturned faces gaped incredulously as the silver ball hung there and dropped no farther. Like the boy with his finger in the dike, I believed I could hold back time by the sheer forces of will, desire, and good intentions. I was encouraged by the knowledge that ancient sailors without clocks had navigated solely by instinct and fortuity.

This room, like the others, has large windows divided into many rectangular panes, thick walls solid straight through, built-in shelves filled with an efficient array of cookware, several sturdy tables, and no chairs. I see now that I am beginning to repeat myself.

In an old barrel with wooden slats and rusted iron bands I found two large clocks, identical in every way. Under normal circumstances, I appreciate an accurate clock but here I tried not to dwell on the fact that these two clocks kept impeccable time.

It was winter. Christmas was coming. I hung clusters of purple glass baubles from the ceiling on strands of invisible thread. This was meant to be festive. Outside, it should have been snowing. But in this part of the world at this time of the year it rains instead.

Each night as dusk fell, I liked to sit on the edge of the table closest to the windows. I would roll up my shirt sleeves, eat my toast, and sip my sweet milky tea. Sometimes it was raining, cold drops on black asphalt. On Christmas Eve, children sang carols in the street, their faces and their voices cherubic under red and green umbrellas in the rain. I was smug, thinking myself exempt from the passage of time, the wretched welter of loneliness, the annoying need to question, insist, or explain. Despite all the evidence against me, I was not afraid. It was easy enough to be brave with these purple walls wrapped like the robes of royalty around me.

On New Year's morning I awoke to the sound of a million calendars turning their pages in the wind. I was forced to acknowledge the unbearable sweetness of being. You can run but you can't hide.

Now I find myself watching the clocks instead of the rain-sprinkled street. Their faces are impassive but their hands are always in motion. All mechanical clocks depend on the slow controlled release of power. Like the ticking of the clocks, there is a refrain in my head all day long now: *Be careful. Be careful. Be careful.* Sometimes it is only background noise and I am not actually hearing it. But then, if I pay attention to it even for an instant, it drives everything else right out of my head. This is like the way mothers are always warning their rambunctious children: *Be careful, don't fall. Be careful, don't bump your head. Be careful, it's hot. Be careful, it's sharp. Be careful, it's dark.*

When I need to hear a human voice instead of this carnivorous ticking of my brain and the clocks, I talk to the walls. Talking to the walls is not necessarily a bad thing, not if they are good strong walls, perfectly perpendicular, freshly painted, cool and smooth when you press your fevered lips against them. Purple walls in particular can convince you that everything you are telling them is brilliant, witty, and profound.

Time, they say, heals all wounds. Unless of course the wounds were fatal in the first place. He is not Lazarus. He will not rise from the dead. Even time has its limits. Do not expect that your life will follow the orderly unfolding of beginning, middle, and end. Once upon a time our hearts were innocent, generous, and sweet, oh so sweet, sweet hearts. It is time to make it clear that, although hell indeed hath no fury like a woman scorned, still I did not leave his heart to draw flies in the driveway. I did not eat his head first. I did not swallow it whole.

It is time to turn my back on the seduction of these small rooms. It is time to address the issues and answer the charges. It is time to go home: home, where the walls are white and the hearts are black. Oh, do not ask, "Where is it?" *Let us go and make our visit.*

It is time to make it clear that I did not kill him. But yes, oh yes, I wanted to.

BODY LANGUAGE

On a good day (a good day being one on which they do not argue at breakfast, she kisses him goodbye on the mouth at the door before they make their separate ways to work, they have plans for the evening which involve good friends, fancy clothes, white wine, and red meat) his throat goes loose with happiness. His tongue is nimble and lithe. The words flow out of him: clever, witty, and remarkably intelligent. He smiles at strangers on his way to the subway station and laughs aloud with 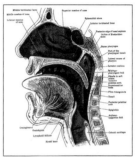 delight at the watery gurgling of a fat baby in a blue stroller. He is confident, fluent, and affable. He could talk all day long to anyone about anything.

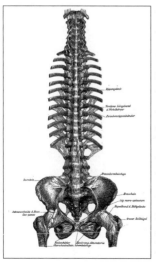 On a bad day (a bad day being one on which she curses him because the coffee is cold, the toast is burnt, the sun is not shining; and she cannot look him in the eye when they leave for work, she says she won't be home till late, she's not sure how late) his throat freezes into formality. He is articulate but icy. His language is laden with precision and good grammar. To his coworkers he says, "Perhaps I shall . . . we intend . . . I assume . . . I spoke with you previously regarding this issue." His sentences are weighted with pompous pauses.

His chest is puffed out with what looks like self-importance but is, in fact, injury. His spine is stiff with offense.

All day long (on a bad day) there is a knot in his stomach, a sour bow of anxiety which tightens and loosens and tightens again as the hours slowly pass. Sometimes it shakes itself free and flows upward to his chest so he cannot fill his lungs with breath, or downward to his intestines which creak and whistle dan-gerously. His coworkers ask him to join them for lunch. He declines in a whisper of mel-ancholy martyrdom. They know better than to ask what's wrong. He will say, "Nothing!" in an accusing voice, affronted by their cu-riosity.

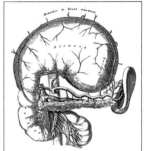

By the end of the day, his stomach is a tight hot drum of gray worry and black bile. It appears slightly dis-tended and he carries it before him like a volatile barrel of toxic waste.

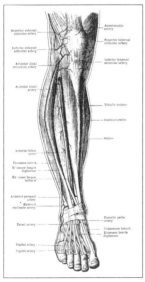

He closes up his office and walks the four blocks to the subway station. He takes no notice of the weather. It could be sunny, it could be raining, it could be a hurricane for all he cares. He pushes past an old lady walking too slowly, elbows his way around a young mother consoling a crying toddler at the curb. He keeps his head down and trudges through the traffic, glaring at the ground. His legs are a pair of aching stumps. His knees alternately threaten to give out or seize up. He stands and waits. He studies his shoes. They are ugly.

He takes a seat on the train and crosses

his numb legs primly. A woman sits down beside him but shrinks into her side of the seat and looks away. Perhaps he is muttering to himself. Perhaps he is moaning softly as he clutches his knees with both hands.

The house when he gets there is empty. Although he has expected this, still he goes from room to room searching. The kitchen is ominously immaculate, as if it will never be used again. Every surface shines, as if even the fingerprints have been wiped clean. The living room is a well-appointed museum, entirely free of clutter, dust, and oxygen. He goes upstairs. Only the bedroom is in disarray, the sheets and blankets in a rumpled pile, three of her silk blouses tossed among them, her white night-gown discarded in a puddle on the floor, her earrings scattered sparkling across the top of the black dresser.

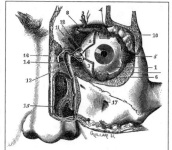

In the bathroom he faces himself in the mirror. He opens his eyes as wide as he can and still he cannot see her.

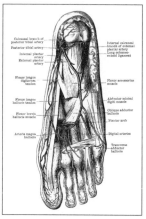

On a good day, she would have been home before him. If they have planned to have dinner out, she is already getting dressed when he arrives. She asks his opinion on her outfit. She suggests other possibilities, holding each up against herself and sashaying through the bedroom. He tells her they are all perfect, the shimmering expensive dresses that cling to her slim body, sliding over her like water when she moves. They are all perfect: how can he ever decide? Downstairs in the living room they have drinks and discuss the day. They put on some music and sometimes they dance. Once she places her little feet on top of his and holds tight to his neck while he waltzes her around the room like a child at a wedding. Even on a bad day, he will always remember this: her little hands, her little feet upon him.

Or (on a good day) she would have been in the kitchen starting supper with the radio on, humming and chopping and stirring. He puts down his briefcase and takes off his shoes (which are not so ugly on a good day). He hangs his suit jacket carefully in the front closet next to hers. In the kitchen he gratefully discovers that she is making his favorite pasta. In the kitchen he joyfully discovers that she has already changed out of her work clothes and is wearing her black silk kimono with the red dragon on the back. She greets him with a kiss. He slides both arms inside her kimono to where her alarming flesh awaits.

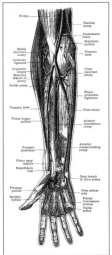

On a good day she lets him.

On a bad day she doesn't exactly push him away but turns, gracefully, out of his embrace like a ring once stuck on a finger magically re-

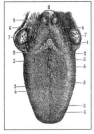

moved with soap. Both her skin and her kimono are slippery and he cannot hold on. He is left with his arms hanging empty at his sides, then braced hard against the kitchen counter to keep himself from grabbing her, begging her, forcing himself upon her. He tries to console himself with the thought that all relationships have their ups and downs.

But on a good day the black kimono slips from her shoulders and then she puts her tongue in his mouth.

He doesn't exactly want to make love. What he wants is comfort. What he wants is to lay his head between her breasts, plump breasts, marvelously heavy breasts on such a small body. He wants to close his eyes and press his lips against them. He wants to bury his nose in them and suffocate with pleasure. He wants to hold his ear against them one by one and listen to her heart beating, her blood flowing, like the ocean inside a seashell. But he is afraid to tell her this.

Perhaps she would think he is weak. Perhaps she already thinks he is weak. Perhaps he *is* weak.

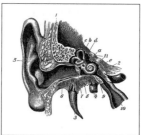

They make love. Then they eat pasta with clam sauce. They drink red wine, toasting themselves liberally. They make small talk and are happy.

On a bad day, when the house is empty, he hangs up her blouses and her nightgown. He puts her earrings back in the jewelry box. He makes the bed, moving woodenly around it, as quietly as if she were sleeping and he must not wake her. He removes his clothes and lies down naked on the bed. He presses his ear to the pillow. He will wait here until she arrives and then he will ask her where she's been. Yes, he will ask her. Finally he will ask her. And she will answer.

Finally she will answer, and finally the flute-edged silence which surrounds them will be filled with the truth.

But for now the only sound is that of his own blood throbbing in his ear.

He doesn't mean to fall asleep but he does, and quickly, exhausted by anxiety. He does not dream. He does not move a muscle. He awakens instantly at the sound of the front door opening. Is it her or is it an intruder? Either way his heart is pounding and his ribs are aching as if he has been thoroughly kicked by a horse or a pair of steel-toed boots.

He thinks of the Bible story, God causing Adam to fall into a deep sleep, then removing one of his ribs and closing his body up again. No mention made of which rib, which side, or whether Adam missed it. Then God created Eve from Adam's rib: Eve, bone of his bones, flesh of his flesh. *And the man and his wife were both naked, and were not ashamed.*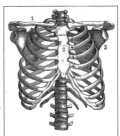

He hears her humming as she takes off her jacket. She calls his name. She sounds happy, excited, girlish. He is relieved, even though her good mood likely has nothing to do with him. She calls his name again. Somehow it does not occur to him to answer. He looks at the bedside clock and finds he has been asleep for only forty-five minutes. She is hardly late at all. He hears her coming up the stairs.

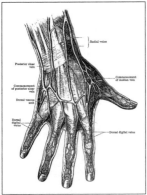

If she is surprised to find him naked on the bed at this early hour, she does not say so. She lies down beside him and slips her hands between his legs. Her hands are cool and very small. Her diamond rings catch lightly in his pubic hair. He sighs. Her fingers are like the stems of young flowers. His hands upon her are clumsy and large. His thick gold wedding band shines.

He doesn't mean to respond. He means

to be cool, logical, mature, rational, and philosophical if necessary—none of which are states of mind that may, generally speaking, be achieved or sustained while making love. He means to remain in control of the situation. He means to speak to her as he spoke to his coworkers earlier: "Perhaps I shall . . . we must . . . I presume . . . I intended to consult with you earlier regarding this important issue." Her breath all over him is sweet and fermented, as if she has been recently sipping expensive liqueurs. He means to ask her about that too. He means to speak to her. He means to make her speak to him.

But slowly, slowly his penis grows hard under her little hands, her little tongue, her hard little teeth. Slowly, slowly his large body betrays him and he cannot help but enter her. They have not had sex for two weeks.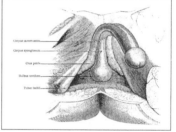

Afterward she goes back downstairs and starts her supper preparations. He has a shower and gets dressed.

If she has a lover (he is pretty sure she has a lover but he has not asked her, will not ask her, at least not today) then maybe he should get one too: thrust and parry, tit for tat, an eye for an eye, and all of that. There is a woman at work who flirts with him all the time: at the 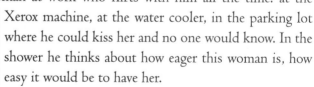 Xerox machine, at the water cooler, in the parking lot where he could kiss her and no one would know. In the shower he thinks about how eager this woman is, how easy it would be to have her.

But he is afraid that if he sleeps with this woman, he will discover that between her legs she is exactly like his wife. Or nothing like her at all. Either way he could not bear it. Either way he would be humiliated and his body would turn away from her, stunned and soft.

Getting dressed, he imagines his wife in the kitchen below. He pictures her as he always does, one perceptible part at a time. Ankle, elbow, that small round bone protruding at the wrist, cheekbone, jaw-bone, left temple with one blue vein showing, the nape of her neck, her collar-bone like a turkey wishbone, her hands in 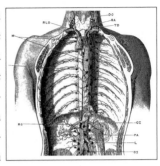 her lap, silent. He has to admit that he cannot imagine who she is when he's not with her, who she is when she's alone. He has no idea what resides within that small body, all of these parts joined seam-

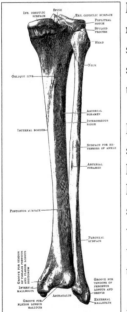

lessly together to produce *her*: this one woman, a mystery without precedent or duplicate, entirely singular: *her*. When he tries to understand her, she escapes him entirely. The heart of the mat-ter is no longer visible to his naked eye.

He can feel it in his bones: her restlessness, her silence, her moodiness, her guilt, and sometimes her fear. He does not know if she still loves him. If not, he does not know when she stopped. He wonders what you do with love when you're done with it—where do you put it, where does it go, how do you make sure it stays there?

He can feel it in his bones. They wake him in the night, the long strong bones of his legs, not exactly aching or cramping, but shrinking, sinking, dissolving, and draining away.

He can feel it in his bones: the future.

Eventually he will have to get it through his head.

For now, as long as nobody speaks the words aloud, he can concentrate instead upon the language of her ankles, elbows, that small round bone protruding at the wrist.

Eventually he will have to get it through his head.

But for now, he need listen only to her body, near him, humming. For now they will make small talk and be happy.

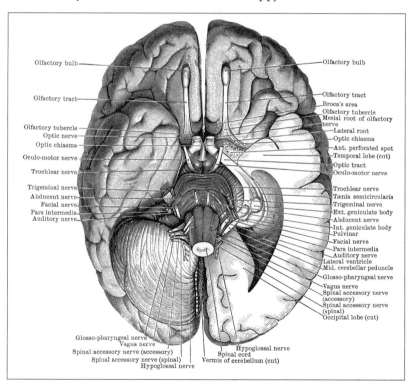

INNOCENT
OBJECTS

The burglary took place sometime between the morning of Friday, July the seventh, and the late afternoon of Sunday, July the ninth, while Helen Wingham was away in the city. Helen went to the city every summer early in July. *(The thief is watching the house.)* The timing of her trip was arbitrary, this particular part of the season chosen for no particular reason, at least not for any good reason that Helen could remember now. She hired a town boy to come out and water her garden while she was away.

She took the Friday morning bus and sat for the two-hour trip south in the window seat behind the driver with her small hands folded in her lap. *(The thief is walking through the front gate and around to the backyard.)* Through the bus window Helen watched the passage of lush green farmland dotted with white houses, red barns, brown cows, and dirty yellowing sheep. *(The thief is in the garden.)* Helen didn't notice much change in the landscape from one year to the next.

The bus stopped in several small towns much like her own, letting passengers off and on at gas stations or gift shops that doubled as bus depots several times a day. Here change was more evident. Buildings appeared and disappeared seemingly at random. *(The thief is picking peas,*[1] *dropping the crisp stripped pods in a pile in the pumpkin patch.)* A row of derelict wooden houses was bulldozed and replaced by a shiny strip mall. A long green and yellow motel popped up in what had been a cornfield.

[1] American Wonder, the best variety, Helen orders the seeds from a catalogue. The plump green pods hang on delicate vines that curl up the stakes and the chicken wire. Helen likes to eat them raw when they are still young and tender. Later in the season she cooks them up in cream with parsley and pearl onions.

A three-story gingerbread farmhouse was reincarnated as a sprawling stucco ranch-style house with a wall of windows across the front. From the bus Helen could now look right into the living room. She saw a woman in a blue bathrobe walking through the large white room. Helen politely looked away.

Helen Wingham was a fifty-four-year-old woman in a peach-colored silk blouse and a well-cut black skirt. Her short hair was gray and tidy. She wore her reading glasses on a black cord around her neck as if they were binoculars. *(The thief is examining a basket of garden tools accidentally left out on the picnic table.)* By all appearances, Helen Wingham was nothing more or less than a plain white woman. To look at her, you would expect her head to be full of recipes, household hints, gardening tips, knitting patterns, and charming anecdotes about her family.

Helen kept her large handbag on the empty seat beside her so no one would sit there. She enjoyed the bus trip for the time it gave her to sit silently and watch the scenery while, she imagined, certain long-standing, but occasionally worrisome, layers of her personality were being invisibly shed like the miles unrolling behind her. *(The thief is picking a pocketknife[2] out of the basket.)* By the time Helen got off the bus, she expected she would be, if not a whole new person, at least a whole new self.

At home in her small town, she was not sociable either. She did not spend her afternoons sipping coffee in the well-equipped kitchens of other town women. *(The thief is cutting a hole in the screen of the back right*

[2] Ladies Knife with three blades, finest quality steel, German silver bolsters, 4¼-inch stag horn handle. Helen has had this knife for as long as she can remember. She uses it to cut off dead blossoms and leaves in the garden. Sometimes she uses it to cut slugs in half. After her gardening is done, she cleans the dirt out from under her fingernails with the thinnest of the knife's three blades.

basement window which has been left half-open.) The extent of her interaction with them was simply what common courtesy demanded: a polite greeting, a positive or negative acknowledgment of the weather, and, occasionally, a brief observation as to the success or failure of some recent local event or enterprise. Helen supposed, correctly, that she was looked upon as something of an eccentric, standoffish but harmless, surely. *(The thief is reaching in through the hole and unhooking the screen.)* Helen *did* keep to herself, yes, but not in an ominous way, not like those monsters about whom (after human bones have been discovered in the compost pile or else they've gone berserk and poisoned the paperboy and his dog) the unsuspecting neighbors, aghast, feel compelled to say over and over again to television and newspaper reporters, "We never really knew her! She kept to herself but she seemed nice enough! How could we have known?"

Helen had lived alone in the large red-brick Victorian house just north of town for twenty years. Still the townspeople knew next to nothing about her. *(The thief is removing the screen and sliding into the basement which is cool and shadowy after the relentless bright heat of the backyard.)* They knew she had come from a wealthy family, was well-educated, had lived for thirty-four years in the city, then inherited a relative fortune and moved to their small town. She had never been married. She had no children and no pets. Over those twenty years she had had few visitors and apparently no suitors. She lived a very quiet life and bothered no one. *(The thief hooks the screen back in place, wipes off the blade and handle of the pocketknife, and sets it down on top of a large picnic basket.³)* For her part, Helen

³ Woven common elm, middle-hinged lid, brass closures, sturdy handle, gingham-lined. Helen is not sure where this basket originally came from. It is one of those objects that has simply always been there. She has never used it for a picnic. It is filled with junk: old screwdrivers, a baseball shed-

suspected that the townspeople were both provoked by and disappointed in her. She was strange, maybe a little, but not strange *enough*. She was hardly the sort of character from whom small-town legends could be made.

The townspeople had long ago abandoned their secret hopes of a scandal and gone on about their business. "Live and let live, that's what I always say!" That's what they always said when Helen's name came up in casual conversation at the post office or the Sears catalogue shopping counter in the back of the drugstore, at one kitchen table or another, among the women who wondered about her, who wished they knew what her secret was. (*The thief is going up the stairs to the ground floor of the house.*) These women longed to be invited into Helen's house but none of them had ever made it past the front foyer on the few occasions when one of them had come to her door census-taking, selling raffle tickets, collecting money for the Cancer Society or the Salvation Army. (*The thief is in the kitchen.*) The most they could tell from this vantage point was that the house was very clean and the grounds were very tidy, front and back. (*The thief is opening the glass doors of the oak china cabinet.*) Helen, they knew, had neither a housekeeper nor a gardener and they couldn't help but admire her for that.

Mostly Helen's "secret" was whatever enabled her to not need a man (or *them*, for that matter), to live alone for all those years without, so they supposed, having to compromise, capitulate, or provide nutritious meals, clean clothes, and satisfying sex on demand.

---

ding its skin, a coil of copper wire, a broken flashlight, two padlocks without keys, and the guts of an old alarm clock. Helen does not exactly know where this junk came from either. It is as if the old house were quite capable of accumulating such objects all by itself.

For her part, Helen knew these women's faces but not their names, at least not their first names. *(The thief is touching the plates, the bowls, the milk jug, the eight-piece tea service[4] on the middle shelf.)* She knew them as Mrs. Henderson, Mrs. Adams, Mrs. Jensen, Mrs. James. Often she got them mixed up. They in turn called her "Miss Wingham," but among themselves they called her "Helen," with a breezy familiarity they knew they had not earned. *(The thief is running cold water into the shining stainless steel sink.)* Sometimes Helen wished she could give these women what they wanted although she wasn't entirely sure what it was.

Although by all appearances Helen Wingham could have passed for one of them, these women knew in their small-town hearts that she was not. They knew her head was not full of recipes, patterns, or boring stories about her family. *(The thief is filling the copper kettle and placing it on the front right burner of the gas stove where a pretty blue flame leaps up.)* These women knew that by comparison Helen Wingham was exotic and mysterious, forever unfathomable. These were qualities for which they either liked or disliked her, amorphous distinctions which they either envied or begrudged her on any given day.

The bus was rolling through the sprawling outer reaches of the city now. Every year Helen noted how you could be *in* the city for a very long time before you actually got there. *(The thief goes back down to the*

[4] Carlsbad China Tete-à-Tete Set, decorated with a spray of pink roses and green leaves. The set includes teapot, sugar bowl, cream pitcher, two cups and saucers, on a fine china matching tray. Seven of the pieces are in perfect condition but there is a small chip on the lip of the cream pitcher. The set is over a hundred years old and very delicate so Helen seldom uses it except for special occasions like Christmas, Easter, and her birthday, the fifteenth of September.

basement and returns to the kitchen with two large mason jars[5] *and three empty cardboard boxes.)* She took out her makeup case, combed her hair, and reapplied her lipstick while the bus idled at a red light. It was just noon when they reached downtown and the giant office buildings were disgorging slim women in sleeveless dresses and tall men in rumpled white shirts into the shimmering streets. *(The thief takes a box of tea from the cupboard, puts the leaves in the pot, and fills it with boiling water from the whistling kettle.)* The traffic was snarled and slow. Overheated impatient drivers honked their horns impotently, more for effect, it seemed, than with any real hope of accomplishing anything.

Finally the bus lumbered into the depot and Helen and the other passengers got off. She retrieved her suitcase from the belly of the bus and stepped into a taxi which took her to the hotel.

Helen stayed in the same hotel every year. Old but aging well, small but luxurious, it was a three-story gray stone building on a short side street off one of the city's main thoroughfares. *(The thief is sitting at the kitchen table, looking out at the empty road through white lace curtains*[6] *while sip-*

[5] Peach and Pepper Relish: In food processor, chop 2 hot red peppers and 12 sweet red peppers, seeds and all. Add peppers to 12 large peaches (peeled and chopped), 1 cup white vinegar, and 1 teaspoon salt in large preserving kettle. Add 4 lemon halves. Boil gently for half an hour. Remove lemons and add 5 cups white sugar. Boil for another half-hour or until mixture is thick. Bottle and seal. Helen knows this recipe by heart.

[6] Nottingham Lace, single border, *point d'esprit* center with beautiful Brussels effect. Helen washes these curtains (and a similar pair that hangs in her bedroom) by hand twice a year in the bathtub and then drapes them over the shower rod to dry. When she hangs them back up at the windows, they are as soft and fragrant as freshly washed hair.

ping a cup of steaming black tea.) The hotel was rather expensive, even by city standards, but it was well worth it, Helen thought, for the first-class amenities it provided.

The concierge was a handsome older man named Frederick who now greeted Helen by name: "Welcome, Miss Wingham. How good to have you with us again." Frederick stood by while Helen registered and her suitcase was whisked away by a bellhop. *(The thief washes the cup and saucer, then the teapot, and sets them down with the rest of the set beside the mason jars in one of the cardboard boxes.)* Then he escorted her to her room on the third floor.

In the room there was a large soft four-poster bed with a thick white duvet edged with embroidery and white lace. *(The thief is in the hallway.)* There was a silver-wrapped chocolate mint on her pillow and a bouquet of fresh flowers on the bedside table. *(The thief is in the living room.)* In the spotless blue bathroom there was a crystal bowl of potpourri on the marble vanity, a plush white robe hanging from a hook on the back of the door, and a telephone on the wall beside the toilet.

Frederick strode across the room and opened the dark green damask drapes with a flourish. *(The thief sits in the wine-colored armchair beside the bay window, resting both hands upon the white antimacassars spread over its arms.)* Gracious and friendly, gallant in the old-world way, Frederick asked after Helen's health and her general well-being during the intervening year. He was scrupulously polite, never nosy or overbearing.

When Helen first began making her annual trip to the city, Frederick had been a handsome younger man. *(The thief is lifting a small clock*[7]

[7] Cupid's Dart, 6 inches high, finished in bronze with fancy dial and Ansonia movement. Having been largely unaffected by the sting of Cupid's dart in her lifetime, Helen loves her little clock anyway. The fact that it has never kept good time strikes her as fitting somehow in an object of desire. The clock is pretty but

from the mantelshelf of the fireplace.) During one of those early visits, Helen had had a dream about Frederick, an erotic dream in which he had come to her in the four-poster bed and his arms were so strong, his skin so smooth, his tongue so agile, and his penis so amiable and big. She had awakened from the dream writhing, wet, and very embarrassed. For the remainder of that visit, she had avoided Frederick. If he noticed or wondered about her odd behavior, he was of course too discreet to mention it. *(The thief spies a square black typewriter*[8] *on an oak cabinet beside the sofa.)* By the following year Helen had managed to put the dream out of her mind and could act normally around Frederick again.

All these years later she seldom thought about the dream anymore except when Frederick said each year: "Consider me at your disposal, Miss Wingham. I will do anything I can to make your stay a pleasant one. Anything." This was exactly what Frederick had said in the dream as he lifted her nightgown and buried his mouth between her thighs. *(The thief places both hands in position on the keyboard and types:* The quick red fox jumps over the lazy brown dog, *but there is no paper in the machine and the words fall invisible onto the black rubber platen.)* This was exactly what he

---

useless and Cupid's left wing has long since broken off and disappeared.

[8] Remington, all metal working parts and steel type, double case machine writes 78 characters including numbers, symbols, punctuation marks, and fractional figures. The typewriter, despite its advanced age, is in excellent working order except for the sticky letters *m* and *p*. Mostly Helen uses it for letters to lawyers and the like, business correspondence that she feels should be made to look as official as possible. Once she tried to type on it the story of her life but found she did not know where to begin.

was saying now as he backed out the door and Helen thanked him with genuine gratitude both for his courtesy and for everything he had done to her in the dream. Helen and Frederick shook hands warmly and she slid a ten-dollar bill into his palm.

Then Helen unpacked, freshened up, and went downstairs. She took her lunch in the hotel dining room. *(The thief is in the hallway.)* She ordered Gazpacho, Stuffed Mushroom Caps, Asparagus Soufflé, and a small Caesar Salad. *(The thief is in the library.)* At home, if she had lunch at all, it was most often brown toast and tea, sometimes a bagel with cream cheese and some of her own peach and pepper relish. *(The thief admires the books in their shelves, strokes their spines, removes one, flips through it briefly, and then returns it precisely to its proper place.)* Helen marveled briefly at how being in the city always made her ravenous and then she ordered Blueberry Crème Brulée for dessert.

By the time she walked into the street, Helen Wingham had become her city self. She made her way smoothly along the crowded sidewalks, never bumping into anyone or making direct eye contact, bobbing and weaving around slowpokes, ignoring the occasional homeless person camped in a doorway. *(The thief is peering at the pages of a large encyclopedia[9] spread open on a cast-iron bookstand.)* Helen was happy to

[9] The *New Illustrated Universal Encyclopedia: The Book of A Million Facts,* published in Great Britain, 1923, 1,280 pages, including 16 new maps. Helen is fond of skimming through this book for amusing entries. She enjoys "The Modern Household Cookery" which includes recipes for such delicacies as Bone Soup, Sheep's Head Soup, Eggs for the Invalid, Substantial Salad, and Mutton Chops in Ambush. She takes special delight in "The New Household Physician" which, in addition to dispensing information on very serious ailments, also offers remedies and advice regarding such afflictions as Ankles, Weak; Breath, Offensive; Feet, Sweating; Toenail, Ingrowing; and Cramp, Writer's.

see how quickly she adjusted to being back in the city, how she must already look like everyone else around her: purposeful, preoccupied, and completely unapproachable. She felt brisk and confident. *(The thief is in the hallway.)* Navigating the city was like riding a bicycle, making love, or skating: once you knew how, you never forgot. It was simply an intricate series of physical maneuvers which, if performed in the right sequence at the right speed, would carry her safely through. *(The thief is in the music room.)* Although Helen hadn't been on skates or a bicycle since she was a girl, she did not doubt that she could still do these things if she wanted to. *(The thief sits down at the piano but cannot read music and so rests one hand gently on the keyboard and is silent.)* Helen supposed, correctly, that the townspeople would hardly recognize her now.

At home she sometimes felt she was too dreamy, floating aimlessly through the rooms of her sturdy house, anchored to the real world only by the solidity of the house itself and by the high-frequency resonance of the objects with which she filled it. *(The thief looks through the viewfinder of a large brown and black camera[10] into a gilt-framed mirror on the wall opposite the piano.)* Sometimes Helen pictured the roof of her house as a lid which kept her from drifting away entirely, all that lay between her and an attractive pocket of heaven to which she was not yet ready to

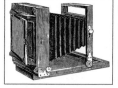

[10] Normandie Reversible Back Camera with adjustable, spring-actuated ground glass always in position, never in the way. Compact, highly polished mahogany body, metalworks of fine-draw file finish. Of course this camera no longer functions. But Helen likes to imagine that if it did, the photographs it took would be like holograms which, if viewed at just the right angle in just the right light, would reveal the whole spectrum of emanations (ghosts of the past, the future, and the truth) which lurk behind even the most mundane surfaces of the present and visible world.

ascend. Sometimes Helen suspected she was hiding, having firmly barricaded herself behind those well-appointed walls, carefully minding her own business and expecting all others to do the same.

Helen arrived at her favorite bookstore. *(The thief is in the hallway.)* It was a long narrow room with floor-to-ceiling shelves that required the use of an old-fashioned ladder on wheels to reach the highest books. The salesclerks wore soft-soled shoes and conservative clothing. They did not bother you unless you specifically asked for assistance. *(The thief is mounting the oak staircase to the second story.)* Classical music played tastefully somewhere near the ceiling.

Helen gravitated first to the biography section. *(The thief stops on the landing and removes a small painting[11] from the wall.)* Although Helen was not generally fond of people in the flesh, she loved to read about them, especially if they were famous in some creative field, especially if their lives had been tormented and chaotic. Although the desire for privacy was paramount in her own life, Helen was thrilled by peeping into the

[11] *Angel of Furnace Ascending* by L. C. Moffat, signed and dated 1891, oil on canvas, 8 × 12 inches, carved wooden frame. Helen knows nothing about this painter, not age, origin, or gender. She thinks though that L. C. Moffat must have been a woman. She intuits this from something in the brushstrokes, which are layered and thoughtful, and from the colors, which are rich and luminous. She does know that Furnace is a small village in the Strathclyde region of western Scotland. But she likes to think this is the angel of *the furnace,* who kindly keeps people warm in the winter. She fancies this notion of the angels of objects: the angels of chimneys, streetlights, and windows; the angels of teapots, cutlery, and kettles; the angels of asparagus, rhubarb, and eggs. These days she especially fancies the angel of doorknobs.

emotional disturbances and scandalous behaviors that pockmarked these famous people's lives. *(The thief looks into several rooms along the upstairs hallway but does not enter any of them.)* Helen was particularly fond of those biographies that included photographs of the subject as a baby in its mother's arms, as a small child in a large class of other unidentified small children, as an unattractive adolescent in a marching band; photographs of the subject arm-in-arm with various spouses and lovers, of the rooms in which the subject had once slept, ate, copulated, and entertained; photographs of the gardens, the children, the pets, the Christmas trees, the birthday cakes, the funeral wreaths. *(The thief is turning the white porcelain doorknob of the last room on the right.)* When reading one of these books, Helen would flip back and forth to these photographs which were, she thought, like the footnotes to the story, the place where all the secrets could be unearthed, the place where the true story could be deciphered and the sum of the subject's life could eventually be tallied.

By the time Helen was finished in the bookstore, she had accumulated enough books to fill three cardboard cartons. *(The thief is entering Helen's bedroom which overlooks the backyard.)* At the last minute she added a five-volume hardcover set called *A History of Private Life* and then she made arrangements to have the boxes shipped to her house early the following week.

Back in her hotel room she closed the drapes against the heat, turned up the air conditioner, and took off her dress. She put on the bathrobe supplied by the hotel and ordered up a light supper from room service. *(The thief is opening the doors of the oak armoire.)* After eating, Helen made herself comfortable in bed, turned on the television, and watched a concert by the Boston Philharmonic. *(The thief is touching Helen's blouses, her dresses, her skirts, and a number of silly-looking hats stored in the bottom drawer.)* After the concert, she turned out the lights and slept soundly, perfectly safe and content, undisturbed all through the summer night, by dreams of Frederick or anyone else.

In the morning she rose early as was her habit, bathed, and got dressed. *(The thief is opening the top drawer of the mahogany dresser.)* She went down to the lobby, greeted the ubiquitous Frederick, and went into the street.

After a half-hour walk through the nearly deserted streets, Helen went back to the hotel for breakfast. *(The thief is touching Helen's panties and a white silk slip.)* Then she spent most of the day prowling through the many antique shops in the neighborhood. *(The thief pulls a leather-bound book[12] from beneath Helen's underwear and finds its blue-lined pages covered with Helen's small neat handwriting.)*

In the early years of her annual trip to the city, Helen had come to these shops looking mostly for furniture. Each year she had bought four or five large pieces and had them shipped home. These beautiful antiques now filled all the rooms of her house. *(The thief opens one by one the four drawers of the mahogany jewelry chest, runs fingers through gold and silver necklaces, brooches, bracelets, earrings, watches, and rings, but does not take anything.)* Helen bought these antiques for the moments of pure happiness they

[12] Hand-bound genuine leather, burgundy and black, bound-in black silk bookmark, best quality white woven paper, 300 pages, ruled. This is not exactly a diary, but rather a notebook Helen has kept sporadically over the last twenty years. The entries are a shorthand notation of her daily life and she often copies into it unusual facts she has come across in her reading. She likes to look back over these selected days of her life. She likes to know that on September 28, 1981, it rained all day, she had pork cutlets, broccoli, and baked potatoes for supper, made an appointment to have the chimney cleaned, and noted that the Pole of Inaccessibility is that point on Antarctica farthest in all directions from the seas which surround it.

offered her each time she walked into a room and: there they were! Every day the sheer sight of them would give her a jolt of surprised satisfaction. It was like catching sight of her own reflection now in a store window as she walked through the city streets. *(The thief takes a large photo album*[13] *out of the glass-fronted bookcase by the window.)* Glimpsing that cosmopolitan woman striding along with such graceful determination, Helen thought, "Now there's a fine-looking woman!" just in that split second before she recognized herself.

But much as Helen loved her possessions, she had to admit that sooner or later even the most extravagant objects of her affection would become just furniture after all. *(The thief hears noises outside, a bicycle perhaps being leaned up against the house, footsteps coming down the driveway and passing into the backyard below.)* Then she went back to the city and bought more. After ten or twelve years of this, even Helen's big house contained just about all the fine furniture it could hold. *(The thief stands just*

[13] Blue Plush Album with photo of six children under celluloid on front, tinted interior pages with floral decorations in gold, openings for 48 photographs. Helen bought this album complete nearly fifteen years ago. The people it contains are perfectly dead strangers. All she knows of them are their names noted neatly on the back or below: *Gertrude and Walt, Janey and Little Luke, Charlotte and Tiny (dog).* Sometimes more details are given: *Lindsay at cabin, Blackstone; Edith on holiday, England; Maurice on his twenty-first birthday at the Chateau.* Every picture is a mystery. Every eye, every elbow, every dish, every drawer, each and every innocent subject and object waits to spill out its secrets like pearls. Helen is still waiting to receive them.

to the right of Helen's bedroom window looking down at the town boy as he unrolls the hose and begins to water the garden.) Now Helen scoured the antique shops for smaller treasures, precious bits and pieces of long-dead strangers' lives which she could then make her own, all of their history there for the taking, all of their dreams there for the imagining.

Today she found, among other things, a miniature toy harp with seventeen tunable strings; a man's alligator-skin traveling case still containing comb, toothbrush, razor, and strop; an eight-ball croquet set with fancy striped mallets and copper-plated arches.

Then she went back to the hotel and had a nap, suddenly exhausted after all that shopping in the heat. *(The thief steps back from the window and sits motionless on the edge of Helen's bed until the boy gets back on his bicycle and rides away.)* She spent the evening much as she had the night before. But tonight she did not fall asleep so quickly.

Tonight she lay awake for a long time, happily buoyed up by a burgeoning sense of possibility. *(The thief stands up and smoothes the wrinkles out of the white eyelet counterpane with both hands which are trembling slightly.)* Here in the city Helen was emboldened. Here she felt she could do anything that crossed her mind. Anything. Here she still believed her life could change. It was not too late. Any day now she could wake up and find herself living a totally different life.

At home Helen did not like to contemplate change. *(The thief goes back downstairs to the kitchen.)* There she was comforted by the sameness of her solitary days. She valued stability, security, and peace of mind. She avoided anyone and anything that might cause anxiety, confusion, disappointment, or overstimulation. *(The thief sets the three full cardboard boxes in the back hall.)* At home when Helen thought about the future, she hoped simply to find herself living exactly the same life for the rest of her life. *(The thief goes into the backyard, unrolls the hose, and turns it on a small flower bed that the town boy had overlooked.)* Sometimes at night Helen's hope took the form of a prayer: "Please God, just let me be."

But here in her hotel room she lay awake for hours imagining herself in all manner of new and startling situations. *(The thief leaves by the back door, making sure it is locked afterward, carrying the boxes one at a time to a gray midsize car parked a hundred yards down the road, pulled onto the shoulder under a clump of weeping birches.)* She could travel. She could visit the Parthenon, the Eiffel Tower, the Pyramids, the Sphinx. She could take a slow boat to China. She could sell the house and buy a villa in the south of France. For that matter, she could *keep* the house and *still* buy a villa in the south of France. She could redecorate in Danish modern. She could dye her hair red. She could write a book. She could take flying lessons. She could get married, for God's sake!

But in the morning Helen did none of these things. *(The thief, on the final trip to the car, is passed by a brown station wagon with two crying children and a barking dog in the backseat, and the harried woman at the wheel does not notice or wonder about this familiar-looking person carrying a cardboard box down the country road in the sunshine.)* In the morning Helen rose much later than usual and enjoyed a sumptuous brunch in the hotel dining room. She sat for a long time sipping her coffee and sampling the bountiful offerings of the dessert table.

Having finally eaten her fill, Helen went upstairs and took her clothes from the armoire, her toiletries from the marble vanity, and repacked her suitcase, removing all traces of herself from the room.

Her bus home did not leave until three o'clock. *(The thief is driving slowly away, down the country road and into the center of town.)* She went downstairs to the lobby which was decorated to resemble an old-fashioned parlor with overstuffed armchairs, antique lamps on well-polished tables, deeply worn Turkish carpets on the hardwood floor. *(The thief pulls into the driveway of a bungalow with pale yellow aluminum siding and black trim, red and white geraniums in the window boxes, two well-pruned cedar bushes on either side of the front door.)* In fact the hotel lobby resembled Helen's living room at home which she had begun to long fondly for now. She was always glad to go to the city but always glad to get home again too. It was exhilarating, all this feeling adventurous and confident, exhilarating but exhausting, and she was looking forward to turning back into her essential dreamy comfortable self.

In the lobby Frederick asked if she had enjoyed her stay. Yes, of course she had, she always did, everything was wonderful. *(The thief opens the yellow metal door with the remote control gadget in the car and drives into the garage.)* They chatted amiably about nothing and then, as the time of Helen's departure approached, Frederick had the bellhop bring down her suitcase while she checked out. He carried the suitcase into the street and hailed her a taxi. Again they shook hands warmly, looking forward, they both said, to next year, and Helen slid him another ten-dollar bill.

The bus ride home seemed, as always, to pass more quickly. *(The thief carries the boxes one at a time into the kitchen of the bungalow.)* Helen watched the scenery unraveling now in reverse as the city peeled off her like a sunburn. She thought about all her purchases and was immensely satisfied.

By five o'clock Helen Wingham is unlocking her own back door and stepping gratefully into her own back hall. She leaves her suitcase there, the door unlocked, and goes into the kitchen, grinning. *(The thief unpacked the three boxes and lined up the objects on the kitchen table.)* Helen finds it reassuring to see her own self reflected in each and every object, and beyond herself, there are the reflections of all the other hands which have touched them, all the other lives with which these innocent objects have intersected over time. *(The thief opened one of the mason jars with a pop, took a large spoon from the cutlery drawer, sampled the peach and pepper relish, declared it delicious, and put the jar in the refrigerator.)* Oh it is so good to be home!

The house is hot and stuffy, having been closed up tight since Friday. *(The thief made room for the other jar of relish in the cupboard to the right of the sink and arranged the tea service on its tray beside the cookbooks on the counter.)* Helen opens the kitchen window and puts the kettle on to boil. She takes the everyday tea things from the cupboard and a tiny spoon[14] from a wooden rack on the wall.

She sits at the kitchen table, looking out at the empty road through the white lace curtains. *(The thief fiddled with the Cupid mantel clock but was disappointed to find that it could not be made to keep good time.)*

Rejuvenated, Helen lugs her suitcase up to her bedroom. *(The thief went into the living room.)* She opens the window and looks out over the garden. The town boy has obviously done his job well. All the vegetables and flowers look robust and vigorous. She can see there are some beans that need picking and the peas are definitely done. *(The thief, having no fireplace, no mantelshelf, placed the clock on the coffee table beside a candy dish in the shape of a fish and a large arrangement of plastic flowers.)* Helen unpacks her

---

[14] Solid sterling silver, 5 inches long, souvenir of Venezuela, palm trees and oil well on handle, the word *Caracas* engraved in tear-drop bowl. This spoon is one of a collection of twenty-four which Helen bought, complete with oak display rack, just last summer. Her favorites among them, besides Venezuela, include Pisa with a braided handle featuring the famous Leaning Tower itself, El Salvador with palm trees and a man on a mule (no whisper of unrest), Wales with a castle on the handle and the coat of arms embossed on the bowl. Helen likes having souvenirs from places she has never seen and surely never will.

suitcase and puts her things away. She notices that the right door of the glass-fronted bookcase is standing slightly ajar. Inside, all the photo albums on the middle shelf have toppled over. *(The thief surveyed the corners of the living room through the viewfinder of the camera and then placed it on the coffee table beside the clock.)* When she opens the door to straighten them, Helen realizes that the blue plush album is not in its proper place. This is most unusual.

Helen turns and looks all around the room. She can't remember the last time she looked at the album. She checks the other shelves in the bookcase, the bedside table, inside the large trunk[15] at the foot of her bed. She even lifts up the white eyelet counterpane and checks under the bed.

She panics briefly, thinking of premature senility, wasn't there a cousin with Alzheimer's, what were the signs? *(The thief went back into the kitchen and rummaged through the junk drawer looking for a hammer and a nail.)* Helen reassures herself by reciting the Ten Commandments. Thou shalt not kill. Thou shalt not commit adultery. Thou shalt not steal. Thou shalt not covet. Her memory appears to be intact.

She is hot. She is tired. She is hungry. *(The thief removed a framed print of Van Gogh's* Sunflowers *from the wall behind the couch, hammered in a new nail, and hung the angel painting there.)* Maybe there is the beginning of a

[15] Fancy metal-covered flat top with rounded corners, hardwood reverse bent slats, metal bumpers. There is nothing of consequence in this trunk: two wool blankets, a linen tea towel printed with a 1964 calendar, a cushion covered with a picture of Niagara Falls, a collapsible walking stick with a dog's head on top, and a black cashmere shawl which Helen has never worn. Usually she sits on this trunk while she puts on her panty hose each morning.

headache behind her eyes. Maybe later, when she feels better, she'll find the photo album.

For now she will put away her suitcase and have something to eat. There are some bagels in the freezer, some cream cheese in the fridge. She goes down to the basement for a jar of peach and pepper relish. *(The thief sat down on the couch and turned the pages of the photo album, peering into the faces of stiff-backed strangers posed beside plant stands, grand pianos, and miscellaneous pets.)* Helen could have sworn she had two jars of relish left. But there is only an empty space on the shelf where they should be.

Helen is beginning to feel anxious. She imagines the jars of relish, the photo album, all the other objects in her house, the books, the tables, the dressers, the rolltop desk, and the rocking chair[16], everything rearranging itself in her absence in some macabre dance of the inanimate.

Then she sees it. *(The thief looked for a long time at the photograph of a stern-faced woman holding a serious fat baby in her lap.)* The pocketknife on the picnic basket. The hole in the window screen. At first she cannot move. Her hands go to her throat. She is suddenly cold in the heat. It does not occur to her that the thief could still be inside. It does not occur to her to abandon her house and run.

She picks up the knife and stares at it. She leans closer to the window. *(The thief picked up the heavy encyclopedia which proved to be filled with all*

[16] Large Oak and Reed Rocker, well-braced, plush tapestry seat. This was one of Helen's first furniture purchases twenty years ago. She sits in it to read in the evening and is invariably comforted by the rhythmic creak of its rockers on the hardwood floor. Once she dreamed she was rocking a baby in this chair. The baby was sucking heartily on her left breast and she was humming a lullaby. In real life Helen does not like babies.

manner of interesting arcane knowledge.) The hole in the screen is a neat vertical cut, a little opening through which her own small hand just fits. She slides the window shut and locks it. She folds up the knife and puts it in her pocket. She goes back up the basement stairs.

In the kitchen now she sees the empty space on the middle shelf of the china cabinet. *(The thief skimmed through several sections of the encyclopedia including "The Dog Lover's Guide With Dictionary of Canine Diseases and Supplements on Domestic Pets, Poultry-Keeping and Bee-Keeping.")* Helen sees that the tea service is missing, but not the brass candlesticks, the Bohemian crystal berry dish, the gold-lined toothpick holder, and not (thank God!) the very rare calling card holder[17] with the bulldog on it. Clearly this thief with the very small hands was an amateur who didn't know the value of antiques. Helen had immediately suspected the town boy, of course, but what could he possibly want with an eight-piece tea service?

Helen feels the remnants of her city self rising to the occasion: she will be practical before she falls apart. She will make sense of what has happened before she allows herself to feel violated, angry, or frightened. *(The thief, in the section called "Encyclopedia of General Knowledge: Essential Facts on All Significant Subjects Clearly Stated and Exactly Defined," looked at photographs of Mount Vesuvius, Stockholm City Hall, and an Australian aborigine armed with three boomerangs.)* Above all else, she will not cry, she will not cry, she will not cry, not yet.

[17] Fancy Quadruple Silver Plated Card Receiver, cast bronze bulldog on base. This is an unusual piece which Helen loves for two reasons. First, because it reminds her of how much better off she would have been to be born in an earlier time when callers came with cards and the world was an altogether more genteel place. Second, because she likes the silly look on the bulldog's ugly face. Despite what other people might think, Helen does have a sense of humor.

Helen walks from room to room assessing the extent of her losses. She knows she should call the police but first she wants to see exactly what is missing. *(The thief opened the leather-bound notebook filled with Helen's handwriting and turned eagerly to the first page.)* Her curiosity is beginning to get the better of her.

In the living room the Cupid clock and the typewriter are gone. In the library she sees the empty stand which had held the encyclopedia. Not one other book is missing. Not one other book is even out of place. *(The thief read the first entry, dated April 26, 1975, obviously written shortly after Helen had moved into the house:* Rain. Lamb chops, peas, mashed potatoes, apple crisp for dessert. Unpacking almost done. Long quiet evening. On the average human head there are 100,000 hairs. They grow 0.01 inches every day.*)* In the music room, only the box camera is missing.

Helen goes upstairs. The angel painting on the landing is gone. She rubs her hand over its silhouette on the wallpaper. *(The thief flipped ahead through the pages and read:* October 20, 1979. High wind, trees moan as their branches are stripped. Leaves to rake tomorrow. Beef stew, too many onions. Can't sleep. Headache. Hire someone to put up storm windows. The seven deadly sins are anger, envy, covetousness, gluttony, lust, pride, and sloth.*)*

Helen looks into each of the rooms along the upstairs hallway but finds nothing amiss. The only sound is that of a dead leaf falling from a large potted fig tree at the end of the hallway.

She goes back into her bedroom. She looks through the jewelry chest. She is relieved to see that everything is still there, especially happy to see her favorite watch[18] which she often wears on a gold chain around her neck. *(The thief read:* January 15, 1983. Snow all day. Meat-

---

[18] Ladies 14K Solid Gold Stem Wind Watch, two diamonds, three rubies, engraved. On the front is the name *Beatrice* and on the back, the inscription *With*

loaf, home fries, creamed corn, and a butter tart. Cozy, reading in front of the fireplace. Perfect silence save for the sound of the flames. The seven virtues are faith, hope, charity, prudence, justice, fortitude, and temperance.)

She looks through her clothes in the armoire and the dresser. She imagines the thief's fingers on her blouses, her dresses, her cool silk slip. She feels to the bottom of her underwear drawer and discovers that her notebook is missing. (*The thief read:* May 24, 1988. Planted geraniums, nicotiana, cosmos, snapdragons, pansies, and six tomato plants. Had hair cut yesterday, also car serviced. Salmon steak, rice, lettuce fresh from the garden. The first woman in space was Valentina Tereshkova who made 48 orbits of the earth in a three-day mission in June 1963.)

Helen knows she should call the police but she cannot bear the thought of them tramping through her tidy rooms, poking at her belongings, fondling all of her precious objects with their big rough hands. She imagines them laughing at her and her thief, both of them inept and eccentric, both of them fools. (*The thief read:* July 28, 1992.

love from Edward forever. When Helen wears this watch, she feels taller, thinner, kinder. She feels like a beautiful woman named Beatrice, much loved by a handsome man named Edward. When Helen wears this watch, she smiles more and is warm toward the women she meets on the streets in town. She laughs with them, admires a new outfit, gives advice on a problem of pests in the garden, lays a hand on an arm while asking after their husbands, their children, their health. These women go home happy to think that maybe Helen Wingham is becoming one of them after all.

Heat wave. Flowers looking desperate though I'm watering twice a day. I was desperate once too but I never knew for what. Water? No. Silence? Maybe. A cloudless shimmering sky. Too hot to eat. Cheese and crackers, carrot sticks, sliced tomatoes, vanilla ice cream. Cannot remember the smell of snow. The ice which covers Antarctica is approximately 6500 feet thick.) Helen imagines the policemen laughing and slapping their knees.

She pulls open the drawer of the bedside table and is relieved to find that the thief has not taken her Holy Bible or her gun.[19] She remembers how, when she bought the gun, the salesman kept assuring her that it was a pure collector's item, had never been fired, not even once. (*The thief read:* September 14, 1994. Spaghetti and meatballs, green salad, garlic bread, cherry cheesecake, one small glass of brandy because tomorrow is my birthday. Make appointment to have furnace cleaned. The heart of a seventy-year-old person will have beat at least 2.8 billion times. Tomorrow I will be fifty-three.)

Helen takes off her clothes and puts on her white nightgown. She knows she should call the police but she cannot bear the thought of the burglary being talked about all over town tomorrow, all those smug women in their kitchens gossiping happily about her and her thief, saying, no doubt, that she had been asking for it, living out there

[19] Harrington & Richardson's Improved Automatic Shell-Extracting Double-Action Self-Cocking Revolver. Nickel-plated with rubber stocks, ebony and pearl inlaid handle. Accurate and dependable, equal to a Smith & Wesson in shooting acumen and power. Weight, 20 ounces; 3¼ inch barrel, 6 shot, 32-caliber, center fire. Helen has never fired a gun in her life but she guesses she could if she had to.

all alone, friends with no one, who did she think she was anyway? *(The thief put down the notebook and rolled a piece of blank paper into the typewriter.)* At the moment she could not have answered this question, parts of her carefully constructed self having been so suddenly stripped away.

She is so tired. She looks down into the backyard. It is not yet dark but the moon is rising, almost full. She will get out there in the morning and pick those beans. *(The thief placed two small hands in position on the keyboard and typed:* This is the story of my life. This is the little story of my little life. Once upon a time there was a woman.*)* But for now she will just go to bed. It is too hot for blankets so she lies down on top of the counterpane with her small hands folded on her chest. She knows she should go downstairs and lock the back door but she does not. She knows she should be frightened but finds that she is not.

She imagines telling this story to Frederick next year at the hotel in the comfortable lobby when he stands close to her and asks how she has been. She imagines how they will laugh, how Frederick will lean toward her and put his warm hand on her bare arm, how she will feel his sweet breath on her face.

(The thief got up from the kitchen table and went out to the garage.) Helen lies very still. She feels very calm.

By the time darkness falls, Helen is almost asleep. *(The thief started the car and backed it out of the garage, out of the driveway, into the street.)*

Suspended between waking and dreaming, Helen sees the bedroom doorknob turning. She cannot decide whether she is dreaming or not. She thinks about the angel of doorknobs. The door is opening. A figure is standing in the doorway, walking toward her. A small hand is reaching out to touch her nightgown, her shoulder, her hair. She can feel sweet breath upon her face. She knows she should be frightened but finds that she is not.

(The thief is watching the house.)

(The thief is walking through the front gate and around to the backyard.)

(The thief is in the garden.)

(The thief is standing in the moonlight looking up at Helen's bedroom window. The night is balmy and bright. The white lace curtains flutter against the screen in the dark. Any minute now the thief is going to call her name.)

Any minute now the thief is going to call her name.

THE SPACIOUS
CHAMBERS
OF HER HEART

The heart, in the adult, measures five inches in length, three inches and a half in breadth in the broadest part, and two inches and a half in thickness. The prevalent weight, in the male, varies from ten to twelve ounces; in the female, from eight to ten: its proportions to the body being as I to 169 in males; I to 149 in females. The heart continues increasing in weight, and also in length, breadth, and thickness, up to an advanced period in life.

—*Gray's Anatomy*, 1901 Edition

Evangeline Clark loved four things, and four things only. Her heart having only four chambers, spacious though they might be, she had limited herself to loving four things.

First there was music.

The **Right Auricle** is a little larger than the left, its walls somewhat thinner, measuring about one line; and its cavity is capable of containing about two ounces.

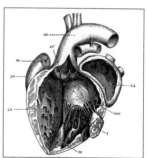

This love she had learned from and shared with her mother who was a pianist, long dead now but still an inspiration to Evangeline. The home of her childhood was always filled with music, her mother at the piano all morning and all afternoon. The meals were slapdash, the house was a mess, but always the air in the cluttered stuffy rooms was saturated with beauty and truth and just plain joy. Sometimes when she had insomnia due to the weight of the world on her slender shoulders, her mother would play Mendelssohn's *Songs Without Words* in the middle of the night and the sound would come gently to Evangeline safe in her little bed, the high notes sprinkling down around her like confetti, the low notes like an August downpour, quarter-sized raindrops on warm asphalt.

At the crucial moment of her life, when she might have become a concert pianist, her mother had become instead her mother. For that was how things were done in those days: one or the other, not both, multiple loves in those days being deemed mutually exclusive. Regret and resentment, like infidelity, were not acceptable maternal manifestations. For this, Evangeline was grateful.

Although she had no musical talent of her own and so had never learned to play an instrument, Evangeline kept the air in her house too always filled with music, any kind of music. There was country and western for hurtin', rock and roll for dancing, jazz for the nerves, blues for the blues, and classical for catharsis. And especially there was Mendelssohn for the middle of the night, to smooth the wrinkles out of the weight of the world.

Secondly there was color.

The **Right Ventricle** is triangular in form, and extends from the right auricle to near the apex of the heart. Its anterior or upper surface is rounded and convex, and forms the larger part of the front of the heart. . . . The walls of the right ventricle are thinner than those of the left, the proportion between them being as I to 3. . . . The cavity equals in size that of the left ventricle, and is capable of containing about three fluid ounces.

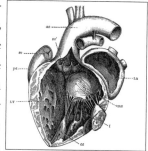

This love Evangeline was learning from and sharing with her husband, who was a painter, a very good painter whose vivid larger-than-life canvases were shown all over the continent. *Brilliant* and *electric* were the words most often applied by the critics, used indiscriminately, it seemed, to describe both the man himself and his provocative and penetrating use of color. Her husband was indeed a brilliant and elec-

tric man, a volatile genius who was always painting in his studio or wanting to. Evangeline quickly discovered that most of the maneuvers and mechanics of daily life struck him as mundane, if not a downright waste of time.

From him she learned that all things, animal, vegetable, or mineral (also plastic, polyester, or nylon), were intrinsically important not because of function but because of color, which is all the naked eye naturally cares about anyway. He spent a lot of time mixing colors, trying to create the true green of grass, the true blue of sky, the true red of blood, and the true ineffable color of the sun, which is not yellow at all, though we have been tricked from an early age into believing that it is. This search for the true color of everything was, he said, like trying to create life in a test tube. But what is life, what is truth, what is the color of your breath in the summer, what is the true color of flesh?

Although she had no artistic talent of her own and so had never painted a picture of anything, Evangeline took great pains to keep her house (his house, their house) full of color. She had a stained-glass window installed in the bathroom so that her husband's naked body (also his naked eye) would glow like an illuminated prism in the shower. This calmed him down considerably because any form of clarity (plain glass, cellophane, Saran Wrap, or water) tormented him unbearably because it was unattainable. She was careful to dress herself in bright colors (yellow scarf, green blouse, blue skirt, red tights, purple shoes) because clearly her husband adored her when she appeared before him like this, with the bands of color encircling her body like a rainbow of pretty ribbons, wondrous bandages from her head to her toes.

Every morning her husband sat in his blue shirt at the breakfast

table, surrounded by the still life she had so carefully arranged: the yellow egg yolks, the red jam, the brown coffee, the purple lilacs on the
windowsill, his red lips, white teeth, chewing and smiling. And while
he admired the orange juice shot through with sunlight, Evangeline
was left breathless and intoxicated with the pleasure of her own power.
Of course she didn't put it to her husband that way. Instead she said
she was smiling because she was happy.

Thirdly there was language.

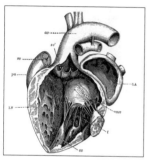

The **Left Auricle** is rather smaller than the
right; its walls thicker, measuring about one
line and a half; it consists, like the right, of
two parts, a principal cavity, or *sinus,* and an
appendix auriculæ.

This love had come to Evangeline of its own volition, right out of the
blue (long before she'd married and discovered the meanings and messages of sky blue, baby blue, the wild blue yonder, or any other mutation of blueness). This love she was sharing with and passing on (she
hoped) to her son who was just learning to read. He followed her
around asking, "What does this say? What does that say?" For every
room, when you looked at it that way, was filled with the printed word.
Besides all the books which covered every flat surface, there were cereal
boxes, labeled canisters, shampoo bottles, toothpaste tubes, postcards,
and notes to herself stuck on the fridge, all of these covered with in-
structions, ingredients, reminders, names, and warnings. He came
home from school with little books which she read to him every
evening after supper. She nearly wept with happiness when he learned

to pick out words by himself: *the, you, go, no, pop, hop, hop on pop.* She printed out lists of rhyming words like *book, hook, took, look, nook, rook, crook, shook,* and they hugged each other with excitement. When she thought about all the words in the language, she had to marvel at the miracle of anyone ever learning to read in the first place. They were all geniuses, when you looked at it that way.

Although she had no literary talent of her own and so had never written a story, a novel, or a poem, Evangeline kept the whole house full of books. There were bookcases in every single room, even the bathroom. The meals were slapdash and the house was a colorful mess, because when Evangeline was not changing the music, or arranging the new purple and turquoise jewel-tone towels in the bathroom,

Ex Libris

she was reading. She had a special little bookstand which she carried around the house with her so she could read while she cooked, while she ate, while she did the dishes, vacuumed, washed the colorful floors. Often she went to bed with a headache (and so had to say to her husband, "Not tonight dear, I've got a headache") caused no doubt by eyestrain. But she preferred to think, in her more whimsical moments, that it was caused by the weight of all the words she'd jammed into her brain, all of them in there whirling and twirling, doing magic tricks, and juggling for position.

Some words were better than others, she knew that by now. All words were not created equal. All words were more than the sum of their parts. A word like *wither* was better than either *with* or *her*, for instance. *Solipsism* was better than either *soul* or *lips*. *Synergy* was better than either *sin* or *energy*. Something was better than nothing. Her overstimulated husband usually grunted and suggested aspirin or therapy but she said she'd rather suffer.

Finally there was light.

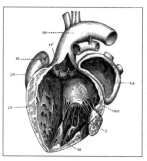

The **Left Ventricle** is longer and more conical in shape than the right ventricle, and on transverse section its cavity presents an oval or nearly circular outline. . . . It also forms the apex of the heart by its projection beyond the right ventricle. Its walls are much thicker than those of the right side, the proportion being as 3 to 1 . . . becoming gradually thinner toward the base, and also toward the apex, which is the thinnest part.

This was her secret love which she had learned from and shared only with herself. For years she had carried it on privately, in love with the muffled pacific light of the bedroom in the morning when it had snowed overnight. Or the amiable pink light of a clear summer morning (which she refused to believe, as her husband warned, was really a result of all the pollution in the dying air). Or the fast-fading light of a midwinter late afternoon which made her legs go weak with lassitude. Or the garish lurid light of a flamboyant sunset, a cliché certainly, but thrilling and unforgettable nonetheless. Or the spring sunbeams on the kitchen floor which her son, as a baby, had liked to sit and smile in like a little Buddha on the green linoleum.

All of these explicit and unconditional lights she had recorded, not with her naked eye, but rather with her naked heart which, she imagined, operated much like a primitive camera, a pinhole in the center through which the illuminated images were funneled and then amplified.

She had read of a university hospital study which determined that women are four times more likely to refuse a heart transplant than men. There must be a good reason for this.

As she grew older, her heart was growing heavier (also longer, wider, thicker) and the spot of light was growing too. This process

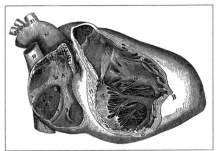

did not require talent. It only required patience and the imponderable passage of time.

Right now, she figured, it was about the size of a regular incandescent light bulb, sixty or maybe a hundred watts.

Soon it would be the size of a spotlight, a perfectly circular beam of lucidity. Then it would mutate into a strobe light, rendering all motion robotic and frenetic. From there it would transform itself into a searchlight, its radiant beacon searching out the secret corners of everything. Next it would expand to the size of a floodlight, washing away all color and confusion within its vast range.

Finally the light of her life would achieve its apex, expanding inexorably and infinitely to illuminate all the spacious chambers of her heart.

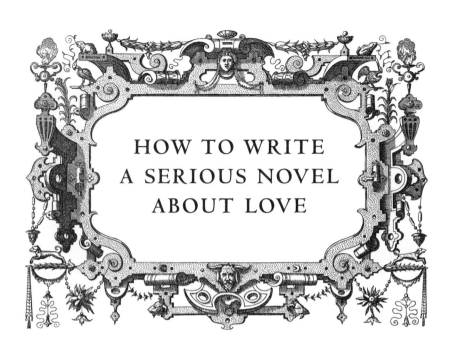

HOW TO WRITE
A SERIOUS NOVEL
ABOUT LOVE

Begin with a man and a woman. Many famous novels begin with this familiar combination. Although it may at first strike you as rather trite, in fact, once you get going, you will find that it presents a vast array of possibilities.

First of all, your man and woman will need names. Consider their selection very carefully. *Vinny* and *Ethel* cannot possibly live out the same story as *Alphonse* and *Olivia*. The reader may well have trouble taking seriously the fates of *Mitzi* and *Skip*. Sometimes neutral names are best. After much deliberation, decide to name your characters *John* and *Mary*. Avoid thinking about John the Baptist, Mary Magdalene, Mary Poppins, or the Virgin Mary. Presumably you are not writing a novel about any of them, not yet.

Describe John.

John has brown hair and brown eyes. John has blond hair and blue eyes. John has black hair and green eyes. John has no hair and no eyes. Pick one. Make John short or tall, fat or thin, pale or rosy-cheeked. Does John have a hairy chest? How big are John's ears, feet, nose, penis? Give some thought to dimples, facial hair, birthmarks, scars, and tattoos. Does John's Adam's apple look like a grape caught in his throat?

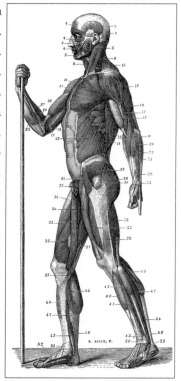

Move from character description to development. John wears gray sweatpants with a hole in the crotch. John wears black, always black, with a black beret. John wears plain white boxer shorts. John wears red bikini briefs. Does John believe in mouthwash, deodorant, foot powder, cologne? What does John see when he looks in the mirror? How does John feel about the shape of his chin, the color of his teeth, the size of his penis?

Do not make John perfect. The reader, who is not perfect, will lose interest. And you, the writer, also not perfect, will lose credibility. Remember, this is supposed to be a serious novel. Above all else, make John human.

Describe Mary.

Again, hair, eyes, height, weight. Be sure the choices you make for Mary coordinate well with the ones you've made for John. How big are Mary's lips, hands, eyes, breasts? Give some thought to cheekbones, crow's-feet, beauty marks, facial hair, and tattoos. How long is Mary's neck? How graceful are her arms when she throws them around John or pushes him away?

Move from description to development. Mary goes barefaced into

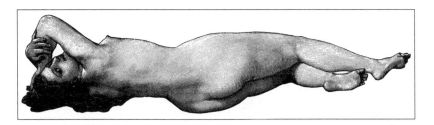

the world, her cheeks scrubbed smooth and shining. Mary spends an hour constructing a new face each morning with a sophisticated battery of potions, lotions, pencils, and brushes. Mary sleeps in a long-sleeved high-necked flannelette nightie. Mary sleeps in the nude. Does Mary shave her armpits and legs? Does Mary shave her legs only to the knee or all the way up? Does Mary believe in cosmetic surgery, aromatherapy, aerobics, vitamins, God? Does Mary have low self-esteem? Does Mary love herself more than anybody else in the whole wide world? Does Mary love herself more than she loves John?

You must describe John and Mary in such detail because readers want to have pictures of them in their heads. Speaking of heads . . .

Decide from whose point of view you will tell the story, into whose head the reader will be allowed access. Decide whose brain you are most interested in picking, whose thoughts will underscore, interpret, and otherwise illuminate the action. This narrator may tell the truth or lies. You decide.

Avoid using the phrase *she thought to herself*. The reader will wonder who else she might have thought to. Remember that no matter how witty, intelligent, or perceptive John and Mary may be, they cannot read each other's minds. If you decide to tell the story through Mary's eyes, remember that she cannot see through walls. She cannot know for sure what John is doing when he is out of her sight. She can only speculate. She cannot even know for sure what John is doing in the very next room, unless of course the walls are very thin. Remember that every point of view harbors its own limitations.

If you wish to dispense with this handicap entirely, choose the omniscient point of view. This narrator, like God, sees all, knows all, and feels free to tell all too. This eye in the sky can see what's happening in Outer Mongolia, Brooklyn, and Brazil, while also being privy to the thoughts of John and Mary and anyone else who happens along. The omniscient narrator also knows the future and the past so be careful.

No matter who is telling their story and/or their future, John and Mary still have to live somewhere. Do not make this decision lightly. Your choice will make all the difference in the world to John and Mary.

If, for instance, you set your novel in the country, its pages will fill up with the smell of freshly turned earth, the growl of tractors and combines, the bleating of baby goats, the twinkling of stars in the vast black sky. The air in the morning will be tinted with the gentle green of trees in

bud. Mary's lips are stained red with raspberry juice. John wears denim overalls and gum boots. They never lock their doors. Mary bakes apple pies in the sunny farmhouse kitchen. John chops the heads off chickens. They sit together for hours on the front porch in straight-backed wooden chairs, peering at the pastoral evening sky, praying for rain.

If, on the other hand, you decide to set your novel in a big city, its chapters will be laced with the exhaust fumes of rush-hour traffic jams, the hum of a million air conditioners, the urgent heart-stopping wail of sirens, the click of high heels on concrete, the grunts and sighs of impatient consumers lined up at ringing cash registers, the slick purr of men and women in power suits conducting high finance in hermetically sealed buildings. At night the office towers glow like radioactive monoliths.

John and Mary live in the fast lane. They work hard to pay for the condo, the alarm system, the cleaning lady, the sailboat, the Christmas vacation in Switzerland. John is a corporate lawyer. Mary is a bond trader. They own a silver BMW. While John drives and curses the traffic all around them, Mary pops open her laptop and sends faxes all over the world.

John starts sleeping with his secretary on Thursday afternoons. This is not very original. After eight months he breaks it off. Mary never finds out. Nothing is changed.

On weekends in the city, John and Mary are always busy. They have many friends but they never have time to see them. They go to films, plays, operas, ballets, art exhibits, and antique auctions. They eat complicated international cuisine in expensive elegant restaurants.

Of course John and Mary know full well that not everyone in the city is as privileged as they are. They know all about the poverty, the crime, the drugs, the homeless, the powerless, the helpless, children abducted and abused, women raped and battered, innocent people murdered for no reason. They see it on the evening news. They read all about it in the morning paper. They are appropriately shocked. Sometimes they see the evidence around them: a man sleeping in a doorway, a bullet hole in a plate-glass window, a bloodstain on a white wall, once the chalk outline of a victim like a hopscotch game on the sidewalk. But they know these things in a haphazard way, the way they know about hurricanes, famine, and war. They see them through a wall of shatterproof glass.

Realizing that you know a lot about city life and virtually nothing about the country, decide to set your novel in the city. After all, you have always been told to write about what you know.

Set your novel in a small old city on the shore of a large polluted lake, a clean respectable city with limestone buildings, heritage sites, sailboats and yachts in the harbor, a prestigious university, a large psychiatric hospital, and several prisons for both men and women. This is what you know. Change the street names to protect the innocent.

Admit that you don't know much about lawyers, bond traders, BMWs, or life in the fast lane. Admit that you have never had a cleaning lady, a sailboat, or a vacation in Switzerland. On weekends you do chores and get groceries at the mall. Then you have a nap.

Make John and Mary ordinary people. Make Mary a teacher. Make John an employee of the railroad. Remember that all ordinary people are extraordinary in their own way. Remember that *ordinary* does not mean *simple.*

If you wish, you may loosely base John and Mary on real-life people. If you are a woman writer, you may base Mary on yourself and John on some man you were once involved with. The real-life John may not appreciate this but then again, he may be flattered to find himself immortalized in print. The reader will enjoy speculating as to the true identities of John and Mary and the small old city in which they live. Later, when interviewers ask if your novel is autobiographical, say, "No, not exactly," and smile enigmatically.

John and Mary may or may not have children. In fiction, as in real life, this is a big decision. Remember that in fiction, as in real life, children are simultaneously miraculous and impossible, with an uncanny power to bring out both the best and the worst in the adults who love them. Remember that in fiction, as in real life, the advent of one or more children into a couple's lives will change absolutely everything.

Always bear in mind that in a serious novel, only trouble is interesting. This means tension, obstacles, conflicts, danger, and desire. This means plot. If John and Mary are happy at the beginning of the book, they must become unhappy later on. By the end, they may be happy again, still unhappy, or else one or both of them may die. A perfectly happy life is, no doubt, a wonderful thing to live, but in fiction it is boring.

Don't forget the villain. Every novel needs a villain. Male or female, make the villain despicable but interesting, vicious but exciting, evil but fond of children and small animals. In a serious novel, the bad guys do not wear black hats. Be careful not to make the villain more interesting than John and Mary.

Although the predominant theme of your novel may be love, it is acceptable and often useful to include subplots which employ one or more of the classical categories of conflict. That is: man vs. man, man vs. nature, man vs. society, man vs. God, and man vs. himself. (Bear in mind that these categories were devised long ago when it was standard practice to refer to all humanity as *man,* so that in each of these constructions *man* also means *woman.* There are no parallel constructions in which *woman* also means *man.*)

In a novel set in the city, it could be very interesting, for instance, to include a version of the conflict man vs. nature. This would allow for a subtext of adventure, danger, and potential heroics to which the average urban dweller does not often have access.

One weekend John goes hunting with his buddies from work. Mary does not approve of hunting. They argue about it beforehand. Mary says that if John brings some dead animal home on the roof rack, she will not clean it, cook it, or eat it. She says she may not sleep with him anymore either. John says, "Fine. Suit yourself." He cleans his gun, stows three cases of beer in the trunk of the car, and dons his jaunty orange hunting cap to prevent being mistaken for a moose and accidentally shot in the head by one of his friends.

On the first day all goes well. None of the men actually kill anything but they have fun tramping through the bush all day and then they drink a lot of beer and tell each other stories of all the other hunting trips they've ever been on. This is called *male bonding.*

On the second day John sets out early while the others are still rolling and moaning in their down-filled bags, sleeping off all that beer. John goes deep into the forest. He hears rustling and snuffling in the underbrush. Stealthily he moves toward the sounds. John's rifle quivers with excitement.

Suddenly a huge brown bear bursts out of the bushes and rears up on its hind legs not six feet away from John. John drops his gun.

He tries to imagine wrestling the bear to the ground with his bare hands. He tries to imagine slitting the bear's roaring throat with the knife he tries to imagine he has in his belt. John has neither the knife nor the courage.

John turns and runs back to camp. For a few minutes he can hear the bear charging through the woods behind him. He imagines being eaten alive one piece at a time. The noises behind him subside and then cease altogether but John keeps running as fast as he can until he reaches the other hunters. He leaps upon the first sleeping bag he sees and hangs on tight. Soon the hunters decide to go home.

Back at home safe and sound, John tells Mary the story of the bear. He shows her the scratch on his right cheek which he says he got when the bear reached out with her giant paw and touched his face, gently, so gently, it was like a caress. In fact, he got the scratch when he was running and a tree branch smacked him in the face. Either way, Mary is not sympathetic. She says it serves him right for hunting. However, she does get out the Band-Aids and the iodine. John tries not to flinch as she cleans the scratch. They have pizza for supper and Mary does not sleep on the couch.

Obviously this scene reveals not only something about nature and bears, but a great deal about John and Mary as well. It is not necessary to state these revelations directly. The reader may resent being hit over the head. In serious fiction, you are supposed to be subtle.

Inner torment is an essential ingredient in a serious novel. The reader will relate well to a character who has emotional problems, who sometimes does not know what she wants, who senses that something is missing from her life but cannot put her finger on exactly what.

Mary has everything a woman could want. She is married to the only man she has ever loved. He loves her as much as she loves him. He is a good provider. He is not physically, verbally, or emotionally abusive. He never forgets to bring her flowers on their anniversary. He never forgets to take out the garbage, hang up the wet towels, or put his dirty socks in the hamper. He vacuums without being asked. They live in a bright, spacious suburban home on a quiet, safe cul-de-sac. They are not wealthy but they are comfortable. They both enjoy their jobs. Their children are healthy, smart, and well-behaved. Mary is a good cook and pursues many hobbies including knitting, stamp collecting, and bowling. John loves golf, swimming, and woodworking. John is a good lover and Mary is often multiorgasmic. Mary has never had a broken heart or any broken bones. Her children do not have allergies or learning disabilities. John does not have high cholesterol or a family history of heart disease. Mary does not suffer from migraine headaches or excessive menstrual pain. Her friends envy her. They say she is leading a charmed life.

Mary knows her friends are right. But still . . . but still . . .

Mary knows she is not as happy as she should be. Sometimes she feels frustrated, dissatisfied, unfulfilled, empty, and bored. Sometimes she gets tired of giving, caring, looking after; tired of wiping counters, tables, noses, and bums; tired of washing clothes, floors, dishes, and her children's hair. Sometimes she even gets tired of washing her own hair. Sometimes she resents always having to be reasonable, reliable, and responsible.

Mary feels the kettle of discontent bubbling inside her. Sometimes she wishes she had become an acrobat instead of the perfect wife and mother. She imagines a skimpy gold outfit with sequins, a thrilling drumroll, the whole crowd holding its breath while she performs death-defying acts before them. She imagines herself afterward, triumphant, riding round the ring on a noble white stallion. The horse's mane and her long blond hair are flowing in the wind. The crowd, roaring, throws flowers and kisses.

Or else maybe Mary wishes she had become an artist. She could have lived in a garret, worn outlandish clothing, and gone to scintillating bohemian parties. She could have taken courses, cruises, lovers of either sex. She imagines her whole head swollen with creativity. After she got famous, her paintings would be hung in exclusive galleries and her openings would be attended by famous people from all over the world.

Now Mary, in her real life, feels trapped. Mary knows that *cul-de-sac* is just a fancy way of saying *dead end*.

In fiction, as in real life, most people want their lives to amount to something even if they're not sure what.

Any minute now the whistle on that kettle of discontent is going to blow. Mary is going to either break out of her own life or get up and make herself a pot of tea.

In a serious novel, such internal machinations may be examined at great length. The more complex the problems, the better the story. Investigate the fears and neuroses of your characters. Make Mary have an anxiety attack in the lingerie shop at the mall. Put John through a midlife crisis. Make Mary afraid of spiders, chickens, horses, fish, tall blond men with beards. Make John impotent. If you are not especially familiar with fears, phobias, neuroses, or impotence, borrow many library books on these subjects. This is called *research*. If the librarian gives you a funny look, tell her you're writing a book.

John and Mary, of course, will both have many memories which occasionally surface within the context of their current lives. In fiction these are called *flashbacks*. Generally speaking, their function is to give your story history and depth. They help the reader understand how John and Mary came to be who they are today.

In fiction, as in real life, a flashback may be triggered by any little thing:

The look of a fried egg on a blue plate, a black umbrella dripping in the vestibule, an old woman in a babushka weeding her garden. The sound of a shovel on pavement after a snowstorm, a song on the radio at the hairdresser's, tires squealing in the night. The smell of shampoo on a strange woman in a crowded elevator, a cigarette lit outside in the winter at night, a woolen jacket in the rain. The feel of a child's hand on your arm, a fat cat in your lap, a silk scarf against your cheek. The taste of an orange, a pomegranate, bitter chocolate, sweet potatoes, the pink eraser on the end of a pencil.

Any one of these things may lead your character back through the doorway of time. The reader will go along gladly into the labyrinth of the past.

In fiction, time is of the essence. In a serious novel, the strings connecting the past, the present, and the future are explicit and articulate. It is only in real life that you may well hang yourself on those same sticky strands. Your readers will likely feel much more comfortable in John's and Mary's past lives than they do in their own.

In fiction, time is finite. Consider how much time your novel will cover: a day, a week, a month, a year, two years, ten, one hundred? All stories must start and end somewhere. The same can be said of individual lives, although not necessarily of time itself. In fiction, as opposed to real life, you control time. It does not control you.

Whenever possible, try to work the dreams of John and Mary into your story. This will elevate your novel above the mundane preoccupations of reality, while handily introducing elements of surrealism, spirituality, and the arcane. For many people, dreams may well be the only remaining indication that there is more to ordinary life than meets the ordinary eye.

Make John dream about turnips, dandelions, an alligator, an accordion, a windmill, and the Shroud of Turin. Make Mary dream about grasshoppers, rhubarb, laundry, an umbrella, a rhinoceros, and a flock of angels descending from heaven and landing in her own backyard.

Give them dreams with music in the background like movies, dreams unrolling like ribbons or a highway, dreams with the smell of cinnamon, sulfur, or gasoline. Give them dreams in which the ordinary continua of space, time, identity, gender, and substance are toppled like towers of wooden alphabet blocks. Give them dreams in which nothing may be taken for granted.

Start dreaming about John and Mary. Say their names out loud in your sleep. Perhaps, if you're lucky, John and Mary will dream about you.

Constructing fictional dreams is trickier than you might imagine. The vocabulary of the dream world bears little resemblance to the common language and landscape of wakefulness. If you find that you cannot make up a convincing dream, then use your own. Put them in the book for safekeeping. Press them between the pages like autumn maple leaves and years later, when you open the book, they will fall into your lap, surprising small wonders, cryptic leaps of faith.

Whether you are writing about the dream world or the waking world, remember to use concrete language. Be specific. Give all objects the dignity of their names. You owe them that much at least.

Avoid vague, limp words like *good, bad, pretty,* and *nice.* Especially be careful around the word *nice.* There is little or no place in a serious novel for a nice man and a nice woman having a nice picnic on a nice day. Even if you say the woman is pretty, the man is good, and the bugs are bad, it is still not enough. You can do better than that.

Especially avoid the use of clichés. If you are going to use metaphors and similes in your novel (of course you are—everybody does), you must search for more original comparisons.

The best way to accomplish this is to lie down in a quiet darkened room and free your mind from the prison of everyday thinking. Forget about the dishes that need doing, the dog that needs walking, the lawn that needs mowing, and your family that needs feeding again and again. Concentrate. Push away the obvious choices, the easy answers.

Dispense with women who are pretty as pictures, with lips like cherries, eyes like diamonds, and skin as white as snow. Dispense with men who are sly as foxes, strong as bulls, quick as whips, thick as bricks, or as slow as molasses in January. Dispense entirely with all of these ideas which are as old as the hills. Instead, train your mind to float away to a higher plane where all thoughts are made new again.

In order to get to the heart of the matter, you must forget all about hearts that look like valentines and pound like hammers.

Go to the place where John's heart is like a piece of celery: crispy, juicy, a pale green stick run through with strings upon which Mary will choke if she's not careful. Go to the place where Mary's heart is like a purse, a soft leather bag in which she carries a jumble of small but vital necessities. When she doesn't need it, she hangs it from the bedroom doorknob.

Go to the place where *love* has nothing to do with hearts, flowers, violins, chocolates, or weddings. Go to the place where *love* is like charcoal, apricots, a helicopter, peppermints, the sound of fingernails on a chalkboard, a bucket of blood under the bed. This is the place where good writing comes from.

Learn to love language. It, after all, is both the tool and the raw material with which you must work. It, fortunately, turns out to be a renewable resource. Make a list of all the words you love and then use them. Words like: *simulacrum, erstwhile, luscious, lunatic, ambush, salubrious, sanctuary, breast.* Do not neglect the power of verbs: *ignite, coddle, holler, galvanize, capitulate, sink, saddle, expire.*

Remember that ordinariness is only in the eye of the beholder. Remember that *ordinary* does not mean *simple* or *dull.* You, as writer, have the power to reveal the extraordinary which lies within (behind, beneath, or beyond) the ordinary. Pay attention to details. Hone your vision. Rekindle the marvel, the innocence, and/or the menace of the mundane. All things have presence. Study the particulars of tables, sidewalks, ceilings, bricks, curtains, crockery, knives. Look out the kitchen window for an hour. See everything. Stare all night at the sky.

If you look long enough at an ordinary cup of tea, it too will become a figment of your imagination. Remember that kettle of discontent about to boil.

Describe the clear hot liquid filling the cup, the white steam rising in the kitchen on a bright March Thursday afternoon. Describe the cup: the white bone china so thin it is nearly translucent, the perfect curves of the handle, the delicate pattern of red and gold  around the saucer. Describe Mary stirring a spoonful of honey into her tea and then licking the hot spoon. Describe the shape of her lips as she takes the first sweet sip and breathes in the aromatic steam with her eyes closed. Describe the sound of the cup being placed carefully back on the saucer. Then describe the silence.

Think of everything you know about tea, about cups, about tea in cups. Think about tea leaves and the future.

Ask yourself why Mary is not at work. She should be standing in front of her Grade Four class right now, teaching them about the solar system, the names of the nine planets in order, the position of the earth in the greater scheme of things. Why is Mary at home? Is she sick? Has she lost her job in the latest round of budget cuts? Has she been fired for insubordination?

Mary, sipping her tea, has a wistful look on her face. Remember that it is possible to feel wistful about almost anything. It is even possible to feel wistful about pain, especially an old pain caused by great love, great loss.

After Mary has finished her tea, she rinses the cup and leaves it on the drainboard to dry. Describe the drainboard and the sound of the warm water running into the stainless steel sink. Think about the fact that warm water makes a different sound than cold water.

Where is John while Mary is having her tea? Mary assumes, correctly, that John is at work. She imagines the train station: the echoing noise of the crowd, all those people crying goodbye and hello, the trains grinding and blowing off steam, the announcements of departures and arrivals, the amplified voice so distorted that no one can understand what is being said but everybody looks up anyway at the high domed ceiling from which the voice seems to emanate.

Mary imagines John looking up at the giant clock on the station wall: it will soon be time to go home. Does John look forward to coming home? Does John come home because he wants to or because he has to? Mary doesn't know and has never thought to ask.

The first thing John does when he gets home is jump in the shower. Mary is studying *The Joy of Cooking* while rattling pots and pans in the kitchen. She is going to try something new tonight: Chicken Tarragon With Wine. She must disjoint the chicken and then marinate it in a mixture of tarragon, shallots, and dry white wine. She will serve it with rice, broccoli, and a fresh green salad. John, she hopes, will be pleased.

John comes into the kitchen. He is wearing a pair of baggy gray sweatpants with a hole in the crotch. He is drying his hair with a thick pink towel. He says, "What's for dinner, dear?"

Mary's mind for a minute goes blank. What is she making? What does tarragon taste like? How do you disjoint a chicken? Who is this man in her kitchen wanting to know what's for dinner, this half-naked man calling her "dear"? Mary stares at John as if she's never seen him before. She stares at the sparse hair on his chest, the muscles in his arms as he rubs the pink towel all over his head.

Mary looks down at John's bare feet on the green linoleum. They are still pink from the shower. His toes are pudgy and his toenails are very small. His baby toes curl inward like plump pink snails.

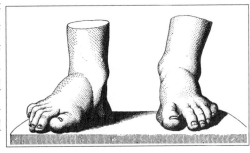

Mary stares at John's bare feet until she understands.

Suddenly Mary knows everything there is to know about this man in her kitchen and, for this brief moment, she can see the future in his feet as if they were a crystal ball. This is called *an epiphany.* It is not clear from the look on Mary's face whether she is disgusted, disappointed, or relieved.

John says, "What's wrong?"

Mary says, "Nothing. Chicken Tarragon With Wine. We're having Chicken Tarragon With Wine."

John says, "Boy, that sure sounds good," and then their lives continue.

Describe the kitchen, the sky outside darkening slowly, the smell of tarragon filling the room. John closes the blinds and sets the table.

Describe the blinds, the place mats, the dishes. Mary makes John put on a shirt before they sit down to eat. Describe the shirt. John says the Chicken Tarragon With Wine is delicious. After dinner, they rinse the dishes and put them in the dishwasher. Then they go into the living room to watch a little TV. It's Thursday. They will watch *Seinfeld* and laugh out loud. Maybe the phone will ring. Notice that John's bare feet make little sticking sounds on the floor as they go down the hall to the bedroom after the news. Take this opportunity to speculate at length as to the nature of love.

Take this opportunity to flex your recently pumped-up metaphor muscles. Think about love as a hot air balloon. Once the lovers have boarded this magical contraption, they will be transported far beyond the reach of the ordinary world. Imagine the earth receding, all of its anger, ambition, and misery reduced to minuscule dots and lines below.

Imagine the breathtaking view. But maybe the balloon will collapse and one or both of the lovers will be forced to parachute back to earth. Don't forget how easy it is to burst a balloon. Don't forget that a person who is full of hot air is not someone you should trust your life to.

Remember that love is blind. This is what you know.

Remember that this all started with an ordinary cup of tea. Look at how far your story has traveled from there. Ask yourself where it will go from here. Remember that as your novel unfolds, you must always strive to create tension and suspense. This is what keeps the reader turning the pages, always wanting to know what happens next. *Suspense* in a serious novel does not mean car chases, killer tomatoes, or a serial killer on the loose. It is also probably better to avoid aliens, UFOs, talking animals, ghosts, and vampires as these elements are seldom appropriate or believable in a serious novel. A murder is okay as long as it is not handled in a spuriously sensational manner.

The building emotion of your story is what will lead the reader forward. Along the way, feel free to run the reader through the gamut of delight, surprise, disgust, anger, disbelief, sympathy, sorrow, lust, and so on.

What the action in your novel must build inexorably toward is called *the crisis.* At this point the various strands of tension and emotion running through your story will come to a head. Although a cataclysmic crisis is more dramatic, it is not absolutely necessary. John and Mary need not end up tearing their own or each other's hair out. Think about the difference between *calamity* and *cataclysm.*

In fiction, as opposed to real life, what follows the crisis is called *the resolution* by which the loose ends of the story are tied up. In a serious novel do not tie up all these ends too neatly. The reader will find this hard to believe because in real life, after the crisis, things just tend to go on and on.

The day will eventually come when your novel is finished. Years have passed. You have tinkered with the commas, deleted the word *nice* seventeen times, worked in all the words you love and then some, words like: *permafrost, paradigm, abacus, sanguine, frugal, stark.* You have rewritten, reworked, and revised as much as you can. You have read the whole book out loud to your cat. You know this novel is as good as it's going to get. You know it's time to stop. On the last page of the last draft, type the words *THE END.* By now these have become the words you love best.

Sit back and admire your manuscript. Tap its many pages into a perfect pile and pat it lovingly. Rest your head upon it and grin. Put your manuscript in a sturdy box and send it to a prestigious publisher. Call all your friends. With any luck, they will take you out to celebrate. Eat shrimp and drink champagne.

For a month or so, believe that you are brilliant. Sit back and admire yourself. Decide what you will wear to accept the Nobel Prize. Watch for the mailman every morning. Resist the urge to kill him when he brings back your novel in its now battered box. Send it out to another (perhaps slightly less prestigious) publisher in a new sturdier box.

Remind yourself that you love writing more than anything else in the world. Read *People* magazine, *National Geographic,* and *The Guinness Book of World Records.* Do not read any other serious novels about love.

Decide to repaint the bathroom. Study the paint chips for days.

Make many trips to the hardware store. Admit that it is a relief to be working with your hands instead of your head. While standing on the ladder painting the ceiling, admit that in your novel about John and Mary you have barely scratched the surface of love. Realize that you know more about love now than you did when you started to tell the story of John and Mary. Some of this new knowledge you have learned from them.

Realize that you have a lot more to say. Think about seismology and the power of love. Feel your veins filling up with words again. Think of all the words you love that you haven't used yet. Words like: *fugitive, iconoclast, wedlock, pendulum, labyrinth, pestilence, shark*. Realize that you will have to write another novel. What else can you do?

Begin with a man and a woman. Many famous novels begin with this familiar combination. Although it may at first strike you as rather trite, in fact, once you get going, you will find that it presents a vast array of possibilities.

A MATTER OF
PERSPECTIVE

The Maya believe that at the beginning of history, when the gods gave us birth, we humans could see beyond the horizon. We were newly established then, and the gods flung dust in our eyes so we would not be so powerful.

—Eduardo Galeano, *The Book of Embraces*

The horizon is a state of mind, an optical illusion, that mythical place toward which we have all convinced ourselves we are traveling. But as we approach it, the horizon is always receding, and the vanishing point becomes the vortex into which we are all longing to be sucked.

It is now common knowledge that the earth is a sphere rotating on its axis while revolving around the sun: yet it remains easier to believe

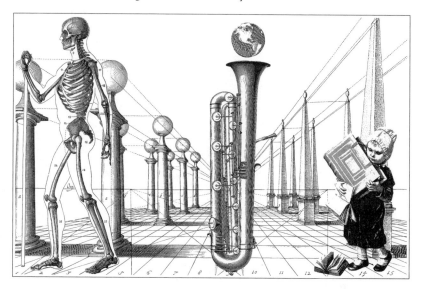

that the world is flat and still. We take perspective for granted, as if we were born knowing that all receding parallel lines must converge at the horizon, as if the vanishing point were the pot of gold at the end of the rainbow. Everything that rises must converge.

It all hinges upon geometry, the hierarchy of points and lines, angles and planes: vertical, horizontal, inclined, oblique, acute, obtuse. The farther away an object is, the smaller it appears. In this context, the word *object* means also the surface of the earth, the sea, the sky, and all living things. In this context, the word *away* also means *ago*. Objects and their reflections always have the same vanishing point. We have been told often enough that seeing is believing but the truth is we can never see things as they really are. It all depends on how you look at it.

Faced with the principles of perspective, I am baffled by the endless task of trying to put things in it. I am plagued by vertigo. I am aging at the same rate as everyone else. I am afraid of becoming one of those people who is constantly asking, "What's the world coming to?" As if they are no longer part of it. As if their hands are tied. The angle of reflection is equal to the angle of incidence.

In an attempt to broaden my horizons, I once traveled alone to a tropical island where the air was warm as bath water, the humidity thick as fish. It bumped against my shoulders and nibbled at my thighs. At home my favorite fish is salmon. As the firm red flesh slides down my throat, I like to think of them struggling upstream to spawn: urgent, primordial, obsessed but not hysterical. Most fish never sleep. They remain always in motion, with their eyes open. But some fish have been known to sleep while leaning on rocks or standing on their tails. To determine the approximate age of a fish, examine the growth rings formed by its scales. Do this before you cook it. The same thing will work for trees but only after you cut them down.

On my trip to the island I was traveling light. I wore the same pink sundress four days in a row. Every night I washed out my panties in the hotel bathroom sink. Every morning they were still damp but I wore them anyway. I wished I'd brought a hat to protect my head from the sun which was closer there and so, naturally enough, larger, rounder, white. On the fifth day I bought a hat from a man in the hotel lobby but it was too late. I was already dizzy all day and at night the bed spun. That big ball hanging over my head had become a constant humming at the back of my mind. Even at midnight the color behind my eyelids was white.

The man who sold me the hat said there had been a massacre on that very spot two hundred years before. He said thousands of natives had been killed but he did not say why or by whom. In these situations, one automatically assumes the aggressors were white. He said there were bones beneath the portico. In my dreams that night there were music and bones, one out of tune, the other out of context. The

music was reedy, the bones were smooth and bleached, like driftwood.

In all directions the horizon was simply the sea meeting the sky. At certain times of the day it was hard to tell where the sea ended and the sky began. At certain times of the day it no longer mattered. Perhaps this was the real reason why I had come to the island. At home the horizon is always obscured by big buildings, tall trees, by memories both good and bad. Even when I stand on my head, still I cannot see it.

On the island in the distance there was often a sound like jet engines revving, an airplane landing or taking off, as if hundreds of people would be leaving or arriving any minute now.

Over my shoulder, a clock was always ticking.

Time has always been the monkey on our backs. Whether too much or too little, too fast or too slow, time is still a one-way street. We can only go forward, we can never go back, except in our minds which, like the weather, the government, and love, are unreliable and frequently exasperating. Time, like gravity, is irrefutable, a clear glass ball rolling down a silver slope. Memory is nothing more or less than the persistent attempt to push that ball back uphill.

I imagine traveling to the home I remember from thirty years ago, only to discover that it isn't there anymore. The spot where it stood is now an empty lot overgrown with dandelions, ragweed, and goldenrod. Someone has dumped an old green sofa and a television set with the screen smashed and its guts hanging out. I sit on the sofa and pretend I am watching *The Ed Sullivan Show* on Sunday night with my parents. The neighbors I knew have either died or grown up and moved away as I did. All their houses are inhabited by strangers who eye me sideways with suspicion. The field where I played softball is now a parking lot. The corner store where I bought romance comics and blue Popsicles from an old lady with her hair in a net is now a fast food outlet. This sort of thing happens all the time. This is the nature of progress.

Everything is smaller, except the trees which are taller but fewer and diseased. The street I was not allowed to cross is now so narrow that when I stand in the middle of it, my outstretched arms nearly touch the parked cars on either side. This too is a matter of perspective. The past, like any other object, has shrunk with distance and the passage of time. This is the nature of nostalgia.

Look back in wonder. Look back as far as the eye can see. All memories have their own vanishing points. I turn my back and walk away. At this point I discover that I have eyes in the back of my head.

Of course I have changed too. I am older, taller, graying, and (supposedly, possibly) a little wiser too. Change is hard for most people. I am no exception. There are still some elementary illusions and expectations which I would gladly cling to if only time would let me.

My own past seems now little more than a tricky act of ventriloquism. Most of the time the present strikes me as a breach of

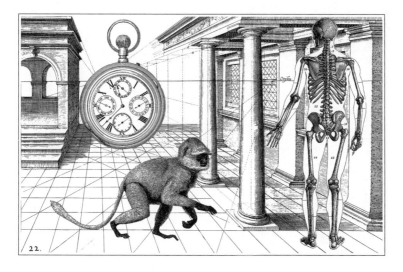

22.

promise. I am not who I was led to believe I would become. And right now I know no more about the future than I ever did.

There must be more to life than the future, more to each present moment than imagining the handsome men we will marry, the grand houses in which we will live, the shiny cars we will drive, the beautiful babies we will give birth to: painlessly, bloodlessly, perfect babies born with their eyes wide open and their dreams intact. We are all approaching the future just as the future is approaching us. We are on a collision course.

Years pass. I try to be patient. I try not to get ahead of myself. A cosmic year is the length of time it takes for the sun to revolve around the Milky Way—approximately 225 million earth years. I wonder how long it will take the future to find me.

My friend Delores had a baby two months ago, a girl, her first. Delores tells me that now she dreams about the baby every night, the baby grown small as a potato or big as a boat. Although she says this in a self-deprecating manner, Delores is very proud of herself and I go sour with envy. I tell her such dreams are probably commonplace

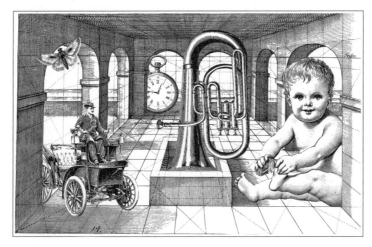

among new mothers. She looks crestfallen. I feel guilty for having rained on her little parade of diapers, breasts, hormones, and maternal instincts. I feel guilty but too jealous to apologize.

At night sometimes I think I can hear the baby crying faintly blocks away. The nights are warm, the windows are open. When I dream about Delores's baby big as a boat, she is clutching a mysterious object in her right hand. When I look more closely, this object turns out to be, variously, an anchor, a roast beef sandwich, or a slippery bar of yellow soap. When I dream about Delores's baby small as a potato, her eyes are sprouting white roots and her smile is inscrutable. There is a clock ticking again, a red one in the shape of an empty uterus.

I wake with a fever and think about how babies will cry if you show them a drawing of a human face with three eyes and an upside-down mouth. Perhaps this explains my lifelong aversion to clowns. It is still dark, the bedroom is crowded with shapeless shadows. I lie in bed and stare at the ceiling: white paint, a few cracks in the plaster, four dead flies in the light shade. The night slips out the window. The sunrise is astonishing.

The horizon is always at eye level, whether you are standing up or sitting down. I wonder where does the horizon go when there's no one there to look at it? Still I cannot see the forest for the trees. Everybody needs something to believe in. When all is said and done, the quality of your life is determined by what and whom you have loved and how much.

We have all been told many times that love is blind. But I have found that this is not strictly accurate. It seems to me that falling in love makes you see things that other people cannot see. Things like: honesty, integrity, wisdom, courage, a future in which you will finally be rich, famous, and happy, a future in which you will finally become the person you have always meant to be. Elevated to a fine clear altitude well above that where all other mere mortals plod on dully through their trivial lives, in love you become a visionary. Anything and everything becomes significant. You are blessed, at least temporarily, with perfect vision. You navigate fearlessly through both the visible and invisible worlds. You have never been more graceful or smart.

When my friends met my latest lover, they were polite but quietly appalled. I could tell. Afterward they cried, "But what do you see in him?" I could calmly list a million things: the faded denim pulled tight across his groin, the angle of his neck as he leaned to kiss me, the sun on his hands as he held out to me a glass of wine, a plate of salmon, a bowl of nuts, a future in which I would finally get what I deserved.

My friends shook their worried heads and asked, "Are you out of your mind?" I smiled coyly and said, "It all depends on how you look at it." This lover's face, it seemed, had always been in the back of my mind, his name on the tip of my tongue. I was through with waiting. I was finally ready to be happy. My friends warned me to be careful but I couldn't see why I should be. They were all happy. Why shouldn't I

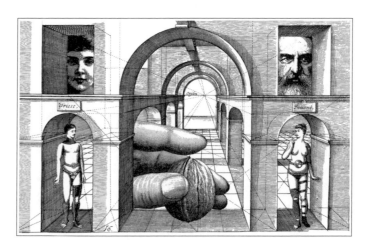

give it another try? As far as I could see, this new lover definitely had potential. As far as I could see, all my dreams were about to come true. I said, "There's more to him than meets the eye."

Our lives, I imagined, were like parallel lines headed arm in arm, neck and neck, toward the horizon where they would ultimately converge and then we would vanish together into the land of happily-ever-after. This was after my trip to the island. The horizon at home being still obscured by structures, foliage, and memories, it was my recollection of that tropical blue meniscus of sea and sky that was my point of reference. I knew neither how to swim nor fly but I didn't perceive this as a problem. I was so enlightened by love that I figured I could do anything. Every night I lay in bed beside him and counted his ribs, like the scales of a salmon, the rings of a tree. I was convinced that if only I loved him hard enough, I would achieve immortality. I was ready to put the horizon behind me. He slept on peacefully while I adored him.

Eventually one of us *did* vanish but not as I had expected.

This new lover proved to be yet another false alarm, another ordinary scoundrel like all the rest who had loved me and left me. Alas, another broken heart. No. The *same* heart, broken again. Still I was not willing to concede that love is blind. Rather, when my friends said (sympathetically), "We told you so," I insisted that love makes you see things that aren't there. Things like: honesty, integrity, wisdom, courage, the future, et cetera. Love is not blindness. Love is a hallucination, the ultimate distortion of reality by which all those parallel lines you've believed in for so long become curves and all perspective is lost. Love lets you loose in a part of the world where the atmosphere is too rare to sustain human life for long. Still you cannot see around the next corner and the horizon becomes a mirage.

You can never see all sides of an object at once. Sometimes there is no time to figure out all the angles. Due to some bad experiences early in life, I am chronically unable to look a handsome man in the eye. I am a master of the sidelong glance. Historically speaking, his smooth skin was nothing but an aggravation of my rods and cones. I am well aware of the imperfections of peripheral vision.

Logic, like beauty, is in the eye of the beholder. I try to draw conclusions the way I was taught to in school. Some valid arguments contain only true propositions:

All tigers are mammals.

All mammals have hearts.

Therefore all tigers have hearts.

Tyger! Tyger! burning bright / In the forests of the night. Where is the forest? How long is the night?

An argument containing false propositions may also be valid:

All birds are mammals.

All mammals have wings.

Therefore all birds have wings.

Ladybird, ladybird / Fly away home, / Your house is on fire / And your children are gone. A bird in the hand is worth two in the bush. Whose hand? Which bush?

Some valid arguments have true conclusions and some don't. Some true conclusions may be drawn from false propositions. The validity of an argument does not guarantee the truth of either its conclusion or its propositions.

To whom should I offer my argument?

My friend Angela suspected that I was having a midlife crisis. She came over to rescue me. She made me a nice cup of tea and patted my hands, my back, my shoulders, my hair. Angela has always been religiously inclined. She said she had been looking into patron saints on my behalf because obviously I could sure use one right now. She figured that, all things considered, my best bet was either Gregory the Wonderworker or Saint Rita, both of whom could be handily invoked in desperate situations. Gregory, who was born in what is now Turkey around A.D. 213, was famous for his spectacular miracles which included changing the course of a river, moving a mountain, and turning himself into a tree. Rita had lived a very tragic life but after her death in 1457 she came up literally smelling like roses and is now invoked against infertility, loneliness, unhappy marriage, and tumors of all kinds. Rita's fragrant body is still on display in a glass case at the Augustinian convent in Cascia, Italy, which, Angela suggested, might be the perfect destination for my next vacation since obviously the tropical island hadn't done me much good.

I listened but said nothing. I stared out the kitchen window. The sun would not stop shining no matter how hard I wished it would rain. My neighbor across the street had a pink plastic flamingo in his front flower bed. I asked Angela if she knew that flamingos are pink because of the shrimplike creatures they eat. Deprived of this food, their feathers will turn white. Angela said she did not know this. But she did know that Saint Gall was the patron saint of birds because he once performed an exorcism on a young girl and the demon flew out of her mouth in the form of a black bird. Lately all of our conversations have been like this one: ridiculous, maudlin, and utterly useless.

Eventually Angela asked me exactly why I was so depressed. I said, "I've been busy putting things in perspective and I don't like what I see." She peered at the tea leaves in my cup until she found a volcano and a piece of lace. The volcano, she told me, symbolized smoldering passions which might erupt at any moment and ruin my life. The lace predicted complicated problems which would cloud my horizon. Angela sees no inherent contradiction in living your life by the leaves as well as by the lives of the saints. As far as she's concerned, you'd better take help wherever you can find it.

Finally she wrote the name of a good therapist in red lipstick on the white tablecloth. She said that, much as she loved me, there was nothing more she could do for me.

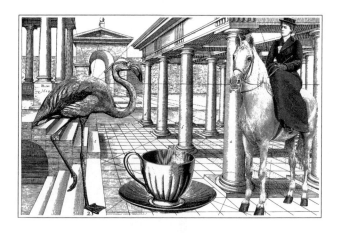

⁂   ⁂   ⁂

All my life I've been on the outside looking in. That's my face at the window, my nose pressed up against the glass. All my life I've believed that someday there would be someone to take me wherever I wanted to go. By now I should know better than to ask for whom the bell tolls.

In retrospect all of my mistakes are clear and close to sublime. It is as if I've been living in a land where all the princes turn into frogs when you kiss them too much. For years I've been trying to figure out the nature of love. This seems to be an unnecessarily well-kept secret. Either everybody else already knows it and they're not telling, or else nobody knows it and they're all bluffing. For years I've wanted to be just like everybody else. For years I've been searching with the sun in my eyes.

I know it's wrong to look at the sun: we've all been warned that we will go blind, our eyeballs will burn right out of our heads. Schoolchildren are kept inside for recess on the afternoon of the solar eclipse. Even they, it is presumed, will not be able to resist the temptation to look.

We are told that the temperature of the sun's surface is 9,900° F.

We are told that we are lucky to be 93 million miles away. Any closer and we would all be burnt to a crisp. Even a diamond will burn if you put a blowtorch to it. At the center of the sun, the temperature is said to be an astonishing 15 million degrees. How can we know this? How can you measure the heat of the sun and survive? Remember the story of Icarus. In early Christian times, a man caught working on the Sabbath was given the choice of being burnt to death by the sun or frozen by the moon.

Owing to the enormous distance from their source of illumination, the rays of the sun are assumed to be parallel. This can only be absolutely ascertained from the perspective of angels.

I am trying now to view my whole life from an aerial perspective. This is like trying to find your own house on an aerial map of the city. From this angle, the vanishing point is nowhere near the horizon and all my petty problems begin to fall away.

No matter how long you think you've been standing still, remember that the earth is traveling around the sun at an average speed of 66,641 miles per hour.

In aerial perspective, shadows in natural light have almost no perspective. From this vantage point, there is virtually no angle of illumination.

The trick is to remember that although the horizon in nature is a curve, we see such a small part of it at any given moment that it appears to be a level straight line. A single object (the object of desire) may hide miles and miles of that line. It may even blot out the horizon altogether. This is due to the distortion called *foreshortening*. The actual size of such an object can only be accurately measured in retrospect. Imagine a blade of grass the size of a palm tree, a fish the size of a zeppelin, a man's head the size of an entire continent. All things are not created equal. Democracy is a form of government, not a standard of living or a matter of perspective.

I have reached the outer limit. It's not that this latest lover was any worse, this broken heart any bloodier than the rest. It's just that I'm tired of doing the same things over and over again while still expecting a different result. I am beginning to understand the mechanics of cause and effect.

I will continue traveling toward the horizon, the vanishing point, and the future. My life will go forward under its own power, propelled by its own narrative momentum. The trick is to remember that the theory of perspective is based on the fact that from every point of an observed object, a ray of light travels in a straight line to the eye. It is not necessary to know the speed of light in order to understand this and change your life accordingly.

I imagine that if I look hard enough (far enough, deep enough, long enough), I will eventually be able to see those lines radiating out from every object at precise angles all the way to the vanishing point. They must be like the strands of a spider web, visible only in a certain light at certain times of the day from a certain angle. You've seen them: those silky filaments strung between branches, fence posts, oc-

casionally right across the driveway or the door. You have felt them on your face in the morning and then brushed them away.

I am learning to live without desire. This brings me to the door-way of uncharted territory. They say the only unexplored area left on earth is the 140 million square miles of the ocean floor. All things considered, I find this hard to believe.

Most of what we think is essential to our survival has been blown out of proportion. I used to think I would die if I couldn't dance. I have finally agreed to stop wanting what I can't have. Everywhere I go, the earth seems to be tilting away from me. If the sun were the size of a basketball, then the earth would be the head of a pin.

I am learning to live with the paradox that the horizon, when I finally get there, is not likely to be at all the way I pictured it.

I fully expect that when I arrive, my equilibrium will be restored and I will be able to traverse the tightrope of the horizon with perfect poise. Then I will know what the world is coming to and why.

Imagine a train traveling straight along the line of the horizon. The plume of smoke from its engine is like a feather against the clear blue sky. I will be on that train, traveling light.

There must be more to life than love. There must be worse things than being alone. Perhaps the trick is to remember that even the angles and shadows of a small empty room must operate according to the protocol of perspective. Examine the absolute inertia of corners where all three right angles must converge.

From my kitchen window I can see brick houses, yellow tulips, my neighbor's pink flamingo, and a blue car traveling north. I can even see the back of an apartment building three blocks over. I can see a small brown bird in a big green tree. I can see those many electrified wires by which we are all connected to each other and to the rest of the world. But I cannot catch even a glimpse of the horizon from here.

I read somewhere once that Cupid was the son of Mars and Venus, the goddess of love. This was later contradicted by another source which said that Cupid's father was actually Mercury, the messenger of the gods. Personally I prefer the first version, that Cupid was fathered by the god of war. This makes perfect sense to me.

The surface of the planet Mars is covered with canyons and volcanoes, the highest of which is Mount Olympus, much bigger than any mountain on earth. For many years people believed there could be life on Mars but now we know that the temperature is too cold and the air too thin. Mars receives enough ultraviolet rays from the sun to kill every living thing.

On Venus the surface temperature has been measured at 890° F even at night. The Venutian atmosphere is almost pure carbon dioxide and the clouds are made of sulfuric acid. Almost all the geographical features on Venus are named after women both real and mythological: Ishtar, Aphrodite, Earhart, Nightingale, Cleopatra, and Colette.

Both Mars and Venus are called *inferior planets.* This is not a value judgment. It simply means that their orbits lie within that of the earth which, according to this scheme of things, is still the center of the universe. From here both Venus and Mars are just two more balls in the sky.

Now that I've finally got all this dust out of my eyes, I discover that I have all the time in the world. The trick is to remember that the horizon, like the future, is always out there: even when it's midnight and you're holding your breath with your eyes closed, even when you haven't been able to catch sight of it for years. The trick is to remember that although, according to the rules of perspective, all receding parallel lines must converge at the horizon, in fact, according to the rules of real life, they don't.

When was the last time you asked yourself:

How hot is the sun?

How old is the moon?

Who invented the wheel?

Who discovered the speed of light?

Who is the patron saint of promises?

What was my first mistake?

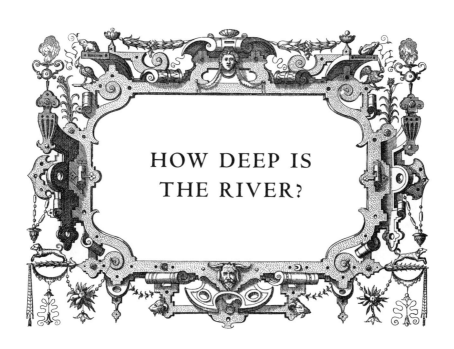

HOW DEEP IS
THE RIVER?

Train A and Train B are traveling toward the same bridge from opposite directions. The bridge spans a wide deep river in which three young women drowned two years ago in the spring. Train A is 77 miles west of the bridge, traveling due east at a speed of 86 miles per hour. Train B is 62 miles east of the bridge, traveling due west at a speed of 74 miles per hour. Which train will reach the bridge first?

(Assume that Trains A and B are traveling on a double track so there is no danger of a head-on collision. Assume that both Trains A and B are mechanically sound, that both engineers are well-trained, well-rested, and have not been drinking. Assume the bridge is well-constructed and meets all federal safety standards. Assume it is August.

Assume that if any of the passengers on Trains A and B are in

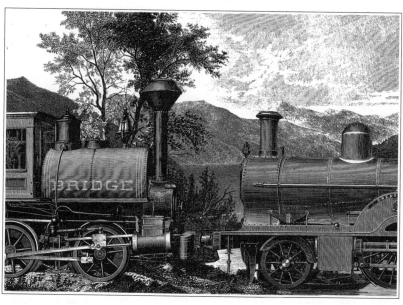

danger, it has nothing to do with their presence here on the shining steel rails approaching the bridge. Assume that nothing bad will happen to any of them during the course of this trip.)

This is like those word problems in high school math, the ones where bits and pieces of supposedly relevant information were given and then a mysterious question was posed.

An elephant's eye is 10.36 feet above ground level. The angle of elevation from a mouse on the ground to the elephant's eye is 46°. How far is the mouse from the elephant?

These knotty problems could only be solved by manipulating the information, making qualified assumptions, and then performing agile feats of arithmetical magic.

A bird is perched at the top of a tree. A cat sits on the ground below. The angle of depression from the bird to the cat is 58°. The cat is 39.67 feet from the base of the tree. How high is the tree?

These problems either caused the mind to go blank or else filled it with other questions, unasked, unanswerable, irrelevant but no less compelling for that. Are elephants really afraid of mice? How hungry is the cat?

Some of these problems were constructed around everyday situations to which high school students were supposed to be able to relate.

When Melanie is shopping, her heart beats about 100 times per minute and she takes 21 breaths per minute. During a trip to the mall that lasts 130 minutes, how many times will Melanie's heart beat? How many breaths will she take? How fast will Melanie's heart beat when she finally finds the perfect shirt which she has been dreaming of for the past three months? (Assume that Melanie has enough money to buy the shirt. Assume the shirt is blue.) How many breaths will Melanie hold while trying on the shirt, praying that it will look as good on her in real life as it does in her dreams?

The solutions to these problems were always in the back of the book. But no explanation was ever given as to how the answers were arrived at, why the questions had been asked in the first place, or what good the solutions could possibly do you once you had them.

Julie is walking west down Markham Street. She stops to wave to her friend Karen, who is leaning out the window of her sixth-floor apartment. The vertical distance between Julie and Karen is 92 feet. The angle of elevation from Julie to Karen is 79°. How far is Julie from the apartment building? (Assume that Julie and Karen are sixteen and seventeen years old respectively. Assume that Karen will not fall out the window. Assume that Julie is wearing her favorite red cowboy boots. Assume it is Saturday morning.) Will Karen invite Julie up for a visit? Will Julie then tell Karen a secret told to her the night before by their mutual friend, Melanie, a secret which Karen promised Melanie she would never ever tell? (Assume that Julie crossed her heart and hoped to die. Assume that Melanie was wearing her new blue shirt.)

Of these three girls, Julie, Karen, and Melanie, which one will get pregnant and drop out of school? Which one will become a veterinarian? Which one will eventually find herself on Train B, 62 miles east of the bridge, traveling due west at a speed of 74 miles per hour?

Train A is full of Friday afternoon travelers. They have all left behind their more or less comfortable homes in City X and are now well on their way to City Y. The population of City X is twenty times greater than the population of City Y. Some of the residents of City X think it is the center of the universe. They are no longer completely convinced that the rest of the country still exists. If it does, they feel sorry for the people who have to live there. They are certain that nothing significant, interesting, or memorable ever happens in the backward barrens beyond the limits of City X. They have never been to City Y. They are not among the passengers aboard Train A as it now approaches the bridge.

Other residents of City X are constantly longing to move away but they are tied there by their jobs, their spouses, their spouses' jobs, or their own inertia. City X suffers from all the social problems indigenous to a metropolis of its size. These problems are now called *issues* and they are running rampant through the streets of City X. Besides all that, the streets of City X are smelly in the August heat and the smog hovers, trapped by a low-lying bank of humidity currently stalled over the city. It is because of these and other more personal issues that some residents of City X are chronically discontent. It is from this portion of the population that most of the passengers on Train A have come. They are so glad to be escaping, if only for the weekend.

What is the ratio of people who love City X to those who don't? (Assume that some people are ambivalent, moody, and unpredictable, loving the city one day while hating it the next. Assume that some people are just never satisfied.) What proportion of those who now love City X will eventually change their minds after one or more of those endemic social issues has impacted directly upon their own lives? What proportion of those who now hate City X will eventually muster enough gumption to leave?

The atmosphere aboard Train A is undeniably festive. Each of its six full cars fairly hums with anticipation and high holiday spirits. Strangers strike up animated conversations, share newspapers, and point out interesting features of the passing landscape: cows, barns, ducks on a pond, once a white-tailed deer bolting gracefully into the bush at the sound of the train. Now this is more like it: no high-rises, no traffic jams, no pollution, no neon, no issues. They are traveling through wilderness now, or at least what passes for wilderness in this overly civilized part of the country. Occasionally their idyll is interrupted by the appearance of the highway, four lanes of blacktop running parallel to the train tracks. The traffic is heavy in both directions, shiny cars and dirty trucks skimming along beside them like little windup toys. Soon enough the highway veers away again and disappears.

On the other side of the wilderness, City Y awaits. Hardly a city at all in comparison to City X, its downtown streets are clean and safe, frequently closed to traffic to allow for buskers' festivals, street dances, and miscellaneous parades. (Assume that if City Y suffers from any of the social issues which plague City X, they are well-hidden and so need not concern the carefree weekend visitor.) City Y rests on the shores of a large lake and much of its summer activity revolves around the water. There are sailing regattas, fish derbies, and free boat rides around the harbor. There is even a beach where the water is still clean enough to swim in. In the waterfront park there are craft fairs, dog shows, jugglers and mimes, hot dog stands, ice-cream carts, and bands playing all day long, some with bagpipes, some without.

None of the passengers on Train A are currently thinking about the bridge, how far they are from it, how soon they will reach it, or about the river, how those poor young women drowned, how the current caught them up and carried them away. The passengers on Train A will simply cross that bridge when they come to it.

Right now the passengers on Train A are thinking about lunch. The food service porter has just begun to make his way down the aisle with his wheeled metal cart. All up and down the car the passengers are pulling out their plastic trays from where they have been quietly nestled inside the padded arms between the seats. Although they are all well aware of the fact that train food is nothing to get excited about, still they smile expectantly at the approaching porter. He skillfully hands out food, drinks, plastic knives and forks, and little packets of condiments from side to side down the swaying aisle.

The porter offers three varieties of prepackaged sandwiches: pressed turkey on brown, ham and cheese on a bagel, and egg salad on white. The beverages available include seven varieties of soda pop, three kinds of juice, three brands of beer, four types of hard liquor, and two kinds of bottled water.

Those who have not traveled by train in some time are surprised to discover that although these sandwiches used to be "a complimentary light meal," now they must be paid for. What remains complimentary are the nonalcoholic beverages and a small package of either salted peanuts or two chocolate chip cookies. How many passengers will now settle for a package of peanuts when they would have had ham and cheese on a bagel if it were still free? (Assume that by the time the porter is two-thirds of the way down the car he will have run out of ham and cheese anyway. Assume that a free dry prepackaged sandwich of any type is much more appetizing than one that costs $3.25. Assume that the porter is pretty well fed-up with listening to people complain about the prices.) If twenty-seven people in this car had ham and cheese on a bagel and seventeen people had pressed turkey on brown, how many people had egg salad on white? Why are there always six egg salad sandwiches left over?

After the basically unsatisfying distraction of lunch, the porter comes around again and collects the garbage in a big black plastic bag. The passengers drop their trays back into their hiding places. Some people order another beer. There is congestion at the very back of the car as people line up for the bathrooms. They stand in the tiny vestibule and look through the glass door at the tracks unrolling hypnotically beneath them. Some of those people staring at the tracks with their bladders full experience a distinct urge to jump. (Assume that everyone successfully suppresses this impulse.) What are the odds that, once any given passenger is finally inside the bathroom and comfortably installed upon the plastic toilet seat, Train A will then encounter a particularly bumpy stretch of track or a sharp curve to the right?

Once the passengers have settled themselves in their seats again, they can get back to contemplating the weekend ahead of them. While visiting City Y, the passengers of Train A will do many different things. Some of them will enjoy shopping for souvenir T-shirts, key chains, and coffee mugs. Others will spend all day in the park eating junk food, while still others will go sailing, waterskiing, fishing, or swimming. They will all enjoy themselves immensely.

(Assume that no one from City X will be mugged, raped, stabbed, hit by a car, bitten by a dog, or spit on by a panhandler while visiting City Y. Assume that no one will be struck down by food poisoning, appendicitis, a heart attack, a cerebral aneurysm, or a severe allergic reaction to seafood. Assume that no one will choke to death on a fish bone. Assume that no one will drown, not in the lake, the bathtub, or a puddle of tears.)

Train B is just as full of festive weekend travelers as Train A. The passengers on Train B are just as happy to be going to City X as the passengers on Train A are to be leaving it. (Assume that this apparent paradox is a manifestation of the notion that the grass is always greener on the other side. Assume that the shortage of grass in many areas of City X is not prohibitive to the exercise of this notion.) Although most of those aboard Train B genuinely enjoy living in City Y, still sometimes they get restless. City Y is so quiet, so safe, so boring, so *parochial*. Some of its residents long for the bustle of the big city, the pulse, the vigor, the culture, the *grit*. While visiting City X, they feel alive again.

Other residents of City Y are not the least bit impressed by City X. These people are utterly convinced that should they ever venture into its congested malodorous streets, some ferocious urban evil would immediately befall them and they might or might not be lucky enough to escape with their lives. What proportion of these people are right?

The passengers on Train B have just been served exactly the same lunch as the passengers on Train A. Their porter has been around to collect the garbage and has scolded several people for changing seats when he wasn't looking. Now the passengers are settling themselves in for the rest of the ride. They are wiggling into more comfortable positions, dozing, or pulling out newspapers, crossword puzzle books, and fat paperback novels by Stephen King and Danielle Steel. Many stare vacantly out the windows, searching still in vain for incipient signs of civilization. Nothing yet: just fields and trees, cows and birds, a cloudless August sky. They sigh impatiently and resume making plans for the weekend ahead.

Depending on their particular predilections, they will partake liberally of the many amenities which City X has to offer. Some of them will shop in malls as big as airports until they are exhausted and broke. Confronted with such a vast array of merchandise, some of them will become overstimulated. Their hearts will beat too fast and they

will hyperventilate while running all their credit cards up to the limit. Others, paralyzed by indecision, will walk away empty-handed, sulky and tearful in a fit of frustrated consumerism.

Some people will spend all day long in museums and art galleries soaking up culture like sponges. In the evening they will dine in expensive restaurants and then go to the theater, the opera, the ballet, or a poetry reading. How many of these people don't really like poetry? How many of them would rather be at a baseball game, a strip club, or an X-rated movie?

Families with young children will go to the zoo, an amusement park, an afternoon show featuring six-foot-tall cat puppets and a man dressed as an elephant playing the violin. How many of these children will pee their pants or throw up while waiting in line to have their faces painted?

The passengers aboard both Trains A and B come from all across the demographic spectrum. This, after all, is one of the beauties of travel. While in transit, people are held in temporary suspension, free for the moment from all the obligations and inhibitions normally imposed upon them by class, race, religion, gender, and by all the doubts they may usually harbor about the rest of humanity. While in transit, people often find themselves telling total strangers things they have not told their best friends.

On Train A, for instance, an elderly woman with blue hair finds herself sitting beside a teenager with green spiked hair and three rings in her nose. They are discussing their favorite brands of hair dye and how hard it is to find a hairdresser you can really trust. (Assume that, although the teenager may eventually dye her hair blue, the elderly woman is not ever going to dye hers green. Assume also that the elderly woman will never have her nose, her tongue, or her nipples pierced.)

Across the aisle, a born-again Christian with a Bible in her purse is assuring an unhappy-looking young man with severe acne and bad teeth that if only he will give himself over to the Lord, all his problems will be solved. How many years will pass before this young man's acne clears up, suddenly, miraculously, without leaving a single scar? How many years will pass before he wins the lottery and uses some of the money to get his teeth fixed and then gives the rest anonymously to the Divine Temple of Supreme Virtue? (Assume that God works in mysterious ways.)

Similarly, on Train B, a gray-haired man in a three-piece suit is listening avidly to an attractive buxom woman with a husky voice describing in great detail her now-estranged husband's reaction to her belated revelation that she had begun her life as a man. (Assume that after years of intensive therapy, the husband will get over it. Assume that the gray-haired man in the suit will not. Assume that he will have erotic dreams about this woman for the rest of his natural life.)

Across the aisle and three rows down, a pale woman in a green dress is pretending to sleep in an attempt to avoid any further conversation with the woman in the mauve blouse beside her. Let the woman in the green dress be Woman A. Let the woman in the mauve blouse be Woman B. Ever since they both boarded Train B at the station in City Y, Woman B has been talking. She is ten years older than Woman A who is the same age now as Woman B was when her youngest child was born. Woman A is five years older now than Woman B was when she got married. How old is Woman A? How long has Woman B been married? Why is Woman A so unfriendly? (Assume that the oldest child of Woman B is the same age now as Woman A was when she lost her virginity. Assume that Woman A was very much in love with the boy who deflowered her. Assume they got married four years later. Assume that this husband of Woman A does not know that she is now aboard Train B on her way to City X. Assume that he thinks she has gone shopping at the mall and will be home in time to make his supper. Assume that until now Woman A has always done what was expected of her.)

While Train B has been steadily approaching the bridge, the river, and City X, Woman B has told Woman A all about the shag carpeting she has just had installed in her living room, the many interesting ways she has found to use cream of mushroom soup, and the colors she intends to repaint the bedrooms in the fall. She has gone on at great length about her husband's midlife crisis two years ago during which he had an affair with his secretary—let the secretary be Woman C— and she, Woman B, pretended she never knew a thing about it until finally her husband got it out of his system and fired Woman C and now their marriage is stronger than ever and they are going to Bermuda at Christmas.

Now Woman A is wishing she had the nerve to tell Woman B to shut up. She can feel the details of Woman B's life bubbling into her ears, filling up her nose, her mouth, her throat, her lungs. She is afraid that if she listens to Woman B long enough, she will either scream or be swept away by the torrent and turn into her. What are the odds that she is right? (Assume that Woman B represents everything Woman A is running away from. Assume that Woman C has her own problems.)

Woman A, the one in the green dress, is Karen, who once waved to her friend Julie from her sixth-floor apartment on Markham Street in City Y. (Assume that years have passed since then. Assume it was Melanie who got pregnant and dropped not only out of school but out of sight as well. Assume the secret Melanie told Julie, who then told it to Karen, was that she had finally gone all the way with her boyfriend, Joe.

Assume this story played itself out in a predictable way: Melanie pregnant, Joe gone, Melanie's parents horrified but anti-abortion, Melanie sent away to a home for unwed mothers, intending to give the baby up for adoption but changing her mind at the last minute, Melanie's parents disowning her, Melanie and her baby never heard from by Karen or Julie again.

Assume that Julie finished high school with good grades, went on to university, moved far away from City Y, and became a veterinarian. Assume that Julie always loved animals.)

Now Karen aboard Train B en route to City X feigns sleep until her garrulous seat-mate nods off herself, snoring lightly with her mouth ajar. Karen opens her eyes and looks out the window. The sky is beginning to cloud over. They are still in the middle of nowhere. If nowhere has a middle, does it also have a beginning and an end? What formula must be used to measure the dimensions of nowhere? What other properties of nowhere can be accurately ascertained? Is nowhere vegetable, animal, or mineral, a solid, a liquid, or a gas? (Assume that nowhere is probably most like water: a shape-shifting liquid which can also disguise itself as a solid or a gas. Assume that no matter in which form it is encountered, nowhere, like water, can be fatal.

Assume it is Karen's penchant for the contemplation of this and other metaphysical questions which has led, at least in part, to her growing dissatisfaction with her quiet normal life in City Y and, sub-sequently, to her purchase of a one-way train ticket to City X. Assume

that her recent realization that her husband is a stupid, boring, insensitive man who is as selfish in bed as anywhere else is also a contributing factor to her defection.)

Karen sits perfectly still and lets Train B carry her forward. She lets all possibility, all promise, all freedom and the future wash gently over her. Ever since those high school days when she lived with her parents on Markham Street in City Y, Karen has been waiting for her real life to begin. Now she imagines that in City X she will find a whole new life and live it, happily ever after. She thinks she will never be bored, lost, or lonely again. She thinks she is going to finally find herself in City X.

(Assume that once Train B crosses the bridge, Karen will imagine it and all other bridges like it bursting into jubilant flames behind her. Assume that Karen will never look back.)

In fact, it is Train A that reaches the bridge first. On the right bank of the river there are four small boys with fishing rods. Considering the heat, the season, and the time of day, how many fish are they likely to catch? (Assume that not one of these boys has ever heard about the three young women who drowned in this river two years ago in the spring. Assume that, as far as these small boys are concerned, there is nothing beneath the surface of the water but many elusive, tantalizing fish and several old tractor tires illegally dumped there by the owner of a nearby farm. Assume that when the boys' fishing lines get snagged, it is on one of these tires, on a rock or a branch, not on a long-dead body still waiting to be raised from the depths.)

Many of the people aboard Train A admire the river, the boys, the quaint and nostalgic picture they make. The boys on the bank wave at the train. The passengers smile and think beatific watery thoughts. They think of floating on their backs with their eyes closed for hours, of warm waves lapping sandy beaches, blue lakes still and clear as windows, aquariums filled with graceful multicolored tropical fish. They think of brooks babbling, a raging thirst quenched, mermaids, sailboats, the sea.

It is only the born-again Christian with the Bible in her purse who thinks about the drownings. She crosses herself and thinks of the four rivers of paradise, the four rivers of hell, the purifying sacrament of baptism, and of how in the olden days those accused of witchcraft were immersed in water and if they floated they were deemed guilty but if they sank they were declared innocent and saved. She imagines the souls of the innocent flying up to the waiting arms of the Lord. (Assume that someday this woman will be one of them. Assume that even now she can feel her wings beginning to grow.)

After Train A has crossed the bridge, it passes Train B which has stopped briefly to allow Train A to safely proceed. Then Train B continues on to the bridge. The boys on the riverbank are still fishing. Again they look up and wave at the train. What are the odds that any of the passengers on Train B are having exactly the same watery thoughts while crossing the bridge as did the passengers on Train A just minutes before? (Assume the observation that you can never step into the same river twice is still true.) What percentage of the passengers on Train B find themselves thinking about sharks, sewage, tidal waves, floods, water on the brain, water on the knee, too much water under the bridge?

Woman B, the garrulous seat-mate of Karen, Woman A, has been awakened by the stopping and starting of the train. The minute her eyes are open, she starts talking again. Why is it not surprising that Woman B knows all about the three young women who drowned? Karen does not want to think about them. Karen wants to think about how, when floating in still water of just the right temperature, you cannot feel your body anymore. Woman B keeps talking, apparently angry at the three young victims for having been so careless, so foolish, so selfish as to go out and drown themselves like that. What were they doing out in that little boat anyway when the river was obviously dangerous, what with the spring runoff, heavy rains the week before, warning signs posted all over the place? Why weren't they wearing life jackets at least? What, she wants to know, what on earth were they thinking of?

(Assume they were not thinking of death. Assume they were thinking of fish, sun, sex, shopping, school, the case of beer in the bottom of the boat. Assume they were not thinking of water as a symbol of both fertility and oblivion, of water as both the source of all life and the end of it, or of the river as the point of transition from one life to the next. Assume that they, like Karen, were thinking they still had their whole lives ahead of them.)

A small boat floats upside down in the middle of a wide deep river which is spanned by a concrete railway bridge. (Assume that someone has spray-painted a crude drawing of a naked woman on the side of the bridge. Assume the drawing is visible only from the river, not from any train crossing over on the bridge.) *How high is the bridge?*

The boat is wooden, white. (Assume that on both sides of the bow are the words JESUS SAVES painted in red block letters.) *How big is the boat?*

On the left bank of the river, Body A is caught in the roots of a tree 33.75 feet from the boat. (Assume this tree in the middle of nowhere is a weeping willow. Assume that Body A will be found first, bobbing facedown in the reeds.) *How old is the tree?*

On the bottom of the river lies Body B. The angle of depression from the boat to this body is 53°. (Assume that soon enough the river will spit out Body B which will then be carted away in a large black bag.) *How many men will it take to lift the bag?*

Body C is nowhere in sight. (Assume that by the time she is found, her hair will have turned into seaweed, her eye sockets will be filled with shells, and her feet will have sprouted silver-green fins. Assume that by the time she is found, there will be no one left to identify her.) *How many miles downstream has Body C traveled?*

The surface of the river sparkles in the sun. (Assume it is disturbed only by fish jumping, ducks diving, the gentle shudder of the wind.)

How deep is the river?

ON LOOKING
FURTHER INTO THE
BODIES OF MEN

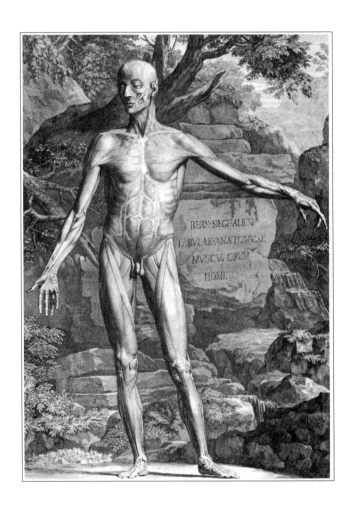

They have their obvious attractions, the bodies of men.

Begin with the neck. The best neck is one slim enough that it does not bring the word *bull* immediately to mind. It should also be long enough to avoid creating the impression that the head is attached directly to the body. Men with no necks are most frequently found in football or hockey uniforms. It is hard to imagine them in regular clothes with collars and ties.

In a good neck the Adam's apple is evident but not pointy. It does not draw attention to itself by protruding too far or bobbling around too much. It should not be scarred from frequent shaving mishaps. The large veins in the sides of the neck are visible but should not bulge except under conditions of extreme stress. Sometimes you can see the blood pulsing in these veins. This should fill you with tenderness, not nausea, repulsion, or murderous intent. Bear in mind that one of these veins is the jugular.

Below the neck are the shoulders which are essential for lifting heavy things like pianos, refrigerators, and the weight of the world. The upper body strength of a man is three times greater than that of a woman. These broad and sensible shoulders are a place custom-made for resting your head on when sleeping, crying, or dancing slow. There is nothing quite like a good set of strong shoulders to make you feel delicate, coddled, and safe.

Also good for crying on is the chest. Many male chests have a little recession in the middle where, if you cry long enough, your tears will collect in a salty pool. The chest should have well-developed pectorals of such definition and muscularity that they cannot be mistaken for breasts. Some men can flex their pectoral muscles individually, making them jump up and down like puppies. This is disconcerting, as are male breasts which are more shapely than your own.

Although men's nipples have no known function, they are attractive in their own way. A chest without nipples would be like a face without eyes.

The issue of chest hair is a matter of personal preference. Usually a chest which falls between the two extremes is the best choice. A completely hairless chest is too slippery and may produce embarrassing sucking sounds when you press your own sweaty chest against it. On the other hand, a thick mat of black fur is not pleasant in the summer. Men whose chest hair sticks out from the tops of their shirts are likely to be inordinately fond of gold medallions, polyester, and pinky rings.

Housed within the chest is of course the heart. Do not assume that a man's heart is essentially the same as a woman's. There are many theories as to the best way to a man's heart. Feel free to try any or all of them but be forewarned that, in truth, this journey remains as much of a mystery as what you are likely to find when you get there. Some men have stones where their hearts should be. Others have holes.

Of the 206 bones in the male body, twenty-four are the ribs, twelve on each side. You should not be able to verify this from the outside. One out of twenty people has an extra rib and this person is most often a man. Be careful about attaching too much symbolic significance to this fact.

The stomach is better without hair and, although it need not look like a washboard exactly, it should not hang over the belt either. If you press your ear to the stomach, you may hear swishing and gurgling sounds like the tide coming into an underwater cave. This could be because the male body contains more water than the female body. Or maybe he's developing an ulcer, to which men are more prone than women.

Below the stomach is the navel which should be tidy and clean at all times. You should be able to stick your finger or your tongue into it without flinching or gagging.

The hip bones should be sturdy but not so prominent as to leave bruises. His bones can withstand stress of 24,000 pounds per square inch but yours may not. The male pelvis is narrower than the female pelvis and more heart-shaped. Forensic scientists have found the shape of the pelvis to be the best indicator of the sex of an unidentified skeleton.

Then there are the genitals. This is the area where most of the commotion is traditionally concentrated.

The average length of an erect penis is six inches. No man likes to be thought of as average. It is better not to mention that the penis of the African elephant weighs sixty pounds and measures six feet in length when erect.

Apparently it is not the size that counts anyway. Marvel instead at the seemingly poreless skin of the penis, and also the color, which is darker than the rest of his flesh, sometimes with a purplish cast. Feel cheered by the way the penis bursts free with such springy enthusiasm from its cage of clothing, as if it will never ever get tired of you.

A penis that bows slightly to the right or the left is endearing. One that seems to nod and wink at you while drooling a single polite drop of semen is enchanting. Many men have pet names for their penises. It is best to tolerate this silliness with equanimity. Do not tell the name to your friends.

Nestled behind the penis is the scrotum. Brown, wrinkled, and prickled with sparse hair, it is the sensitive pouch inside which the testicles lurk. Do not be alarmed by the way the testicles float around inside the scrotum like hard-boiled eggs. It is within the testicles that the sperm are produced. Remember that, while all 400 of a woman's eggs are present in her ovaries at birth, a healthy man will produce 400 billion new sperm during his adult life. It is hard not to admire such industry.

II.

Much as the male torso is tantalizing (evoking, as it does, the image of a treasure chest crammed with mysterious organs, intricate ductwork, and powerful plumbing), the appendages which issue from it are estimable in their own right. They give the male body more range.

You may find it is the arms that you most often long for. The arms with their hard hairless biceps: throwing a ball, lifting a cup, picking up the telephone, shaking the wrinkles out of a sheet. The arms with their firm flexed triceps: reaching out to you, wrapping around you, holding you tight. Pay close attention to the wrists: blue-veined, small-boned, resting on a table, vulnerable, sensitive, and open to interpretation.

Whether the fingers of the hands are long, short, slender, or stubby, they should be gentle but strong. Ideally, a man should have all of his fingers still attached. However, a man who is missing a finger or two will have at least one interesting story to tell. Be wary of hands speckled with scars or too often too quickly clenched into fists. Men's hands are usually warm. This is because the blood flow to a man's hand is greater than that to a woman's. Be suspicious of a man with consistently cold hands. His blood flow may be sluggish and thin. Men with hands like meat hooks should not be dentists, brain surgeons, or magicians.

At the other end of the torso are the legs which should split off from the trunk in a straightforward and symmetrical manner. A severely bow-legged man only looks comfortable when seated on a horse.

Of the 656 muscles in the male body, you may find those in the thigh among the most compelling. A male thigh in motion is a joyous sight to behold. Wrapped around the femur, which is the longest bone in the body, are the sartorius, the rectus femoris, and the vastus, both

externus and internus. These muscles are like flowers: you do not need
to know their Latin names in order to appreciate them. The action of

these large muscles can be enough to make up for any number of other
shortcomings.

Below the thighs are the knees which are seldom attractive and frequently make strange cracking and popping noises. Athletic men of a

certain age are prone to problems in this area. This may lead to many long boring conversations about cartilage, liniment, and famous hockey players whose careers have been ruined by recurring knee injuries. Some men's kneecaps have a tendency to pop out of their sockets. They will expect you to be able to pop them back in again without passing out.

The knee bone is connected to the shin bone, formally known as the tibia. The shins of a full-grown man should not be covered with scrapes and bruises. Unless of course these injuries were incurred while rock climbing, white-water rafting, or groveling at your feet while begging for mercy, forgiveness, and a second chance.

The ankles should be big-boned and strong. Men with weak ankles tend to use this minor infirmity as an excuse to avoid all kinds of physical activity including ice skating, strolling in the moonlight, taking out the garbage, and mowing the lawn.

Attached to the ankles at a 90° angle are the feet. Either you like feet or you don't. After years of abuse and neglect, some men's feet are hideously decorated with bunions, calluses, and corns. The foot contains twenty-six small bones and in some men, all of them are knobby and misshapen. Their toenails may be yellow and gnarled, too thick to be trimmed by normal means. Some men are squeamish and have not cut their toenails properly for twenty years. Often their toes are hairy, their second toes are longer than their big toes, and their baby toes are deformed stubs that look like dead slugs. Men with ugly feet should not expect you to rub, kiss, or lick them. Men with ugly feet should spend a lot of money on socks and shoes which they should then remove only in the dark.

III.

With so much excitement going on in front, the bodies of men are often more restful when viewed from behind.

From this perspective, the nape of the neck is displayed to its best advantage. It, like the wrist, emits an aura of vulnerability and

sensitivity. Herein lies its power. It is best observed by accident when he does not know you're watching him. The sudden sight of the downy nape of a male neck bent over a book in a yellow circle of lamplight will set off a spasm of love in your sentimental throat, your startled heart.

The back itself should be as hairless as possible. Men with hairy backs are frequently embarrassed by this inappropriate hirsuteness. They tend to apologize profusely when taking off their shirts.

A hairless back provides ample opportunity for admiring and exploring an expanse of uninterrupted skin. A single square inch of skin contains 19 million cells, 625 sweat glands, 90 oil glands, 65 hairs, 19 feet of blood vessels, and 20 million microscopic mites. The largest organ in the human body, the skin of an average man covers an area of twenty square feet and weighs about ten pounds. In order to verify this information, the skin would have to be removed entirely and measured accordingly. This is not advisable for amateurs as the procedure is messy and the chances of being able to put it all back on again are slim. It is better to take this on faith, the way you took it on faith for all those years that men were stronger, braver, less emotional, more rational, better at math, and just naturally good with machines.

The skin itself should be smooth and relatively unblemished. Remember that a man's skin, like his blood, is thicker than a woman's. This explains a lot of things.

Running straight down the center of the back is the spine, the largest of its twenty-six vertebrae looking like knuckles, the smallest like peas. On either side of the spine is the latissimus dorsi, the largest muscle in the human body. It is here that you are most likely to catch a glimpse of that legendary rippling effect. At the base of the spine there are often two large dimples which always invite a smile or a friendly kiss.

All men like to have their backs rubbed. This is not an unpleasant activity for either party, but bear in mind that if you do it once, he will expect you to do it all the time. Before offering this service on a regular basis, be sure that he is prepared to reciprocate in kind at least once a week.

The back should taper off gently at the waist. Men without waists can still make good companions but they are harder to slip your arm around when walking down the street. Even men with slim waists frequently have pockets of flesh fondly referred to as *love handles*. These are not always unattractive and can indeed be useful in certain circumstances requiring a firmer grip. Men with very small waists and very broad shoulders have an annoying tendency to strut.

Call it what you will, the male bum is the most frequent focus of attention in the rear view. It may well be the only thing that makes watching professional sports bearable. The gluteus maximus is the strongest muscle in the body and so deserves respect. The bum should be entirely free of pimples and hair. It should not be too baggy, too bulging, or too flat. Men with no bums have trouble keeping their pants up. Whatever the size of the bum itself, the crack should never be exposed above the waistline of the pants. This offensive spectacle is frequently observed in plumbers in your kitchen squatting down to examine the pipes under the sink, and in family men in shopping mall parking lots bending over to put the groceries in the trunk.

The truth is many men look better with their clothes on. This is not a gender-specific trait. It is also true of many women, the difference being that the women usually realize this while the men usually don't.

IV.

The pinnacle of the male body, like the star on top of the Christmas tree or the cross on top of the steeple, is, of course, the head. Some men's heads don't match their bodies. Some small thin men have large fat heads. Some large muscular men have small wobbly heads. Some men with beautiful bodies have ugly heads and vice versa. The problems arising from this type of discordance are largely aesthetic.

The fundamental basis of the head is the skull which is comprised of twenty-two large and small bones. These should be fused together neatly without too many bumps or ridges. This consideration is of particular importance to bald men or those likely to be overwhelmed by a sudden impulse to shave their heads.

Housed within the head are several interesting but potentially problematic features. Not the least of these are the eyes, which should be bright and warm, brimming with promise and virility. Some men's eyes shoot off sparks. Calm yourself with the knowledge that after death all eyes change color, usually becoming a dull greenish-brown.

Some men's ears have hair growing out of the holes in unruly black tufts. You might assume that this is why he never seems to hear half of what you're saying: his ears are plugged with hair. But the truth is that a man's sense of hearing is not as sharp as a woman's. This explains why he never hears the phone ringing, the dog barking, or the baby crying in the middle of the night.

The nose should not be so large as to have you recommending the name of a good plastic surgeon on the first date. It should not be red and bulbous, covered with blackheads, or grossly misshapen from having been broken seventeen times. A nose with some or all of these qualities is a parody of a nose and cannot be taken seriously. The nose should work well, not requiring hourly administrations of nasal spray or endless honking into handkerchiefs. It should also work quietly, without drawing undue attention to itself. Men who breathe loudly are annoying even to sit in the same room with. Men who snore loudly should be informed post-haste that there are now surgical procedures available to correct this problem.

Below the nose is the mouth, a major site of activity and interest. The production of saliva in the mouth should be kept under control at all times. Men who drool and slobber cannot be taken out in public. The lips should be soft and moist, not perpetually chapped and flaking off bits of dead skin. The teeth need not be perfect and pearly white but they should be all there, at least in the front. The tongue should be nimble and not too big. It should not appear to be flopping around of its own free will. You should never look at the underside of the male tongue because it, like the female's, is repulsive. The muscles of the tongue are supported by the hyoid bone which is shaped like a horseshoe and is the only bone in the human body that does not touch another bone. In cases of death by strangulation, the hyoid is usually fractured or crushed and so its condition often provides useful evidence in homicide investigations.

What makes one male head handsome and the next one not remains unclear. There is more to it than the quality and arrangement of these various features. Why the look of one man smiling at you across a crowded room makes you go weak at the knees while the gaze of the perfectly presentable man beside him causes nary a flicker is still one of the great unsolved mysteries of life, like Stonehenge, the Bermuda Triangle, and the disappearance of Amelia Earhart.

The same can be said of the male brain. It, like the male heart, is, by turns, intriguing, alarming, exasperating, and utterly unfathomable. Having completed a thorough examination of the more superficial features of the male body, you will eventually find yourself forced to deal with the brain. You cannot put this off forever.

The male brain, like the female, is not much to look at. A glistening convoluted lump of pale gray matter shot through with red arteries and blue veins, the brain should have tripled in size from birth to adulthood. The size of two clenched fists held tightly together, the average male brain weighs three pounds. The heaviest brain ever recorded weighed 5 pounds 1.1 ounces and belonged to a thirty-year-old man. The lightest brain weighed 2 pounds 6.7 ounces and belonged to a thirty-one-year-old woman. Should any man try to make too much of this, remind him that there is no correlation between brain size and intelligence. Point out that although the male brain is 10 percent heavier, the female brain contains 11 percent more brain cells. The blood flow to the male brain while thinking is smaller than that to the female brain. Some men do not think with their brains anyway.

The capacity of the human brain has been expressed as the number 1 followed by 6.5 million zeros—a number so large it would stretch from the earth to the moon and back again more than thirteen times. Because the brain has no nerve endings, it can be burned, frozen, hit, or sliced without feeling a thing. Each day between 30,000 and 50,000 brain cells die and are not regenerated. Instead they are eaten and digested by other cells. As men age, their brains deteriorate two or three times faster than the brains of women. Although this fact has been documented only recently, it hardly comes as a surprise.

Unfortunately there is no way of knowing anything about a man's brain by looking at his body. When looking further into the bodies of men, the most important thing to remember is that what you see has absolutely nothing to do with what you're going to get.

The brain continues to send out signals for up to thirty-seven hours after death. Brain waves, posthumous or otherwise, are like the wind: you cannot actually see them, you can only see their effects. Imagine a warm breeze wafting through a fragrant field of wildflowers, gently lifting your hair off the back of your neck. Then imagine a tornado scooping up the contents of your heart, ripping it to shreds, flinging the pieces away in all directions at once.

Brain waves are a form of electricity. Imagine a cozy room at dusk, pools of yellow lamplight, the sound of soft music floating on the air. Then imagine sticking your finger in the light socket.

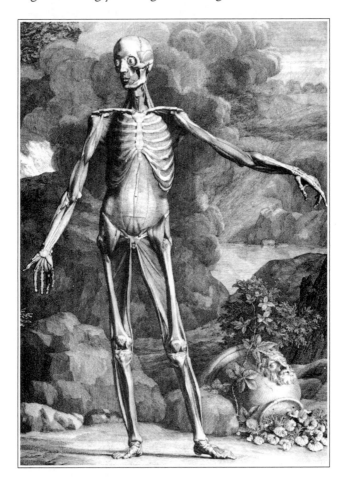

COUNT
YOUR BLESSINGS
(A FAIRY TALE)

Once upon a time there was a young woman named Grace. She was very beautiful. She possessed in ample measure all of the attributes deemed desirable in women of her time. She had a small waist and shapely but not heavy hips. She had generous but not floppy breasts and a flat stomach with a tasteful navel. Her shoulders were graceful and her neck was elegant. She had a clear and healthy complexion, large dark eyes and long dark eyelashes, full red lips and straight white teeth. Her auburn hair was naturally full of body and shine. She also had firm buttocks, long legs, and dainty little feet.

All her life Grace had been told she was lucky. She was told this by her parents, who were obviously proud, and by her friends, who were secretly envious. She was even occasionally told this by total strangers on the bus. Grace knew they were right. Sometimes she would stand naked in front of her full-length mirror and examine herself in detail. She could stand there for an hour or more, counting her blessings. This was not so much vanity as a need to remind and reassure herself of her many assets.

Not surprisingly, young men swarmed around her like sticky-footed flies. For a while Grace enjoyed this very much. She was a romantic young woman who fell in and out of love easily and often. She was certain that someday her prince would come, but in the meantime, not one of these relationships lasted very long. Grace was every bit as discriminating as she was beautiful. Much as each of these many suitors showed great promise in that initial flush of infatuation, soon enough they would reveal their true colors. Soon enough Grace would discover that the current object of her affections was not the man of her dreams after all. Soon enough she would have to admit that he was too moody, too irresponsible, too insensitive, too egotistical, too domineering, or just plain dumb.

There was one young man who, when she told him she didn't love him after all, threw himself at her dainty feet, clung to her pretty ankles, and swore he loved her so much that he would drown himself in her bathwater if she dumped him. But he was also the one who frequently advanced the opinion that a beautiful woman could not be expected to have a brain as well. And so Grace cast him away too, adding yet another broken heart to the growing trail behind her.

Just when Grace was beginning to despair of ever meeting Mr. Right, Cupid finally found her. After all those romantic misadventures, Grace had become, understandably, a little skittish about the whole notion of love. She was more cautious now, less willing to be swept off her feet, a little cynical perhaps, not quite so ready to offer her heart this time around. She had finally realized that most of her previous suitors had been not so much interested in her heart anyway, but rather in the generous but not floppy breasts that concealed it.

But this young man was not like the others. His name was William and he was gentle, sensitive, even-tempered, and intelligent. Although he was obviously well aware of her beauty, he was not obsessed with it and he made it clear that he loved her as much for her mind as any-

thing else. William respected her opinions and was able to admit when he was wrong. He sent her flowers for no reason and took her to romantic movies at which he was not embarrassed to cry when necessary. Grace was very impressed. It did not hurt that William was also very handsome with broad shoulders, a hairless well-muscled torso, a strong jawline, a nice straight nose, and large dark eyes not unlike Grace's own. He also had a good job with a promising future. He was an accountant with a large respected firm and had already been promoted three times in the last two years. But still Grace held back. She was too afraid of being disappointed again. William was persistent, but never pushy. He said he understood her reluctance. He said he had all the time in the world to prove that he deserved her love.

After a year of his patient courtship, Grace had to admit that William was everything he seemed to be, everything she had ever dreamed of. Finally Cupid gave her one last push. Grace saw the light and surrendered. All along everyone had said they were the perfect couple and now Grace realized they were right. William got down on his knees and gave her a big diamond ring. Grace wept with happiness. Her parents were even more obviously proud and her friends were secretly even more envious.

Grace and William began to plan their future together.

The wedding took place six months later at the end of May. As a bride, Grace was more beautiful than ever. She wore a traditional white satin gown with a four-foot train and long full white lace sleeves. In her hair she wore a crown of pink and white sweetheart roses from which a floor-length gossamer veil cascaded all around her. The gown was cut low in the back to a big white bow at her tiny waist. At the wedding ceremony, only one of Grace's friends let envy get the better of her. Upon seeing the white gown, this young woman could be overheard to whisper snidely, "Who is she trying to kid?"

The groom wore a custom-made black morning suit with a black satin cummerbund, a pleated white silk shirt, and a white bow tie. Even the old priest who performed the ceremony and bestowed

his blessing upon them said he had never seen a more beautiful couple.

Grace's mother wept and her father nodded happily as their daughter signed the marriage register with trembling hands. William's parents were equally pleased.

After the ceremony, the newlyweds and their guests ate, drank, and danced for hours. Then Grace and William changed into their traveling clothes and took a rented limousine to the airport. They flew to Paris for their honeymoon. What could be more romantic than Paris in the springtime?

A week later they returned and embarked upon the unparalleled adventure of married life.

In the first year of their marriage, Grace and William made love almost every night and were very busy doing many other interesting things. They were always going to movies, concerts, ball games, and parties. Every Saturday night they went out for dinner. They each had many friends to begin with and now, being such an interesting, amusing, and attractive couple, they made even more. Their phone was always ringing and their calendar was always full.

But after a year or so, they grew tired of this endless social whirl. They were also tired of renting and so they, like many of their friends, bought a large old house and began to spend all their time and money renovating and redecorating. They did most of the work themselves, as was the custom in their circle. Sometimes their friends came over to help.

They learned how to replaster cracked walls, reset crooked windows, refinish hardwood floors, and build simple cabinets and shelves. They scoured antique markets and dragged home battered dressers,

desks, and china cabinets which they then lovingly restored to their former beauty. They learned how to hang wallpaper, lay carpet, and perform minor plumbing miracles.

Each night, after another long day of sanding, painting, hammering, and sawing, they would fall into bed exhausted but proud, as their dream home slowly took shape around them.

✵   ✵   ✵

Of all their home improvement achievements, Grace and William were most proud of the kitchen.

Having agreed that the kitchen was the natural nucleus of any happy home, they spared no expense on its refurbishment. William had recently received yet another promotion so they could afford to go all out. Finally, after weeks of hard work and serious shopping, the kitchen was done, completely reconstructed from floor to ceiling and abundantly outfitted with all the most efficient and attractive accoutrements. Grace and William stood arm in arm in the doorway and admired their creation.

On the large oak table in the center of the room, a white linen cloth glowed, a set of stainless steel bone-handled butcher knives gleamed, and two white antique bowls waited to be filled with finger-licking delicacies and mouthwatering delights. The counter against the right wall was a solid slab of maple two inches thick. There was a complete set of wooden mixing bowls arranged in a tall vertical cast-iron rack, a rare find at an antique market north of the city.

On the back wall there were two built-in ovens, a chalk message board, a brass and mahogany antique clock, and a built-in refrigerator with wooden doors. A second iron rack held five cooking pots of various sizes. A set of copper utensils hung on the wall just below the large casement window through which the sun streamed all afternoon.

The showpiece of the kitchen was a huge cast-iron stove which had been converted to gas. This stove weighed over two thousand pounds and bringing it into the kitchen had required a forklift and six strong men.

The floor, which had of course been reinforced under the stove, was covered in large black and white square tiles. Although the occasion of laying these tiles had involved much cursing and swearing and many mistakes, Grace and William agreed now that it had all been worth it.

Grace made a pot of tea and they sat together in their beautiful kitchen until the sun went down, imagining all the wonderful meals they would prepare here, all the Christmases and birthdays they would celebrate, and in their minds, the future spread out before them like a smorgasbord, a veritable banquet of as yet untasted pleasures, piquant and sweet.

Once the house was finished, there was not much for Grace to do all day while William was away at work. She quickly found that only so much time could be filled with cleaning and rearranging and admiring the splendid contents of the house. She thought about getting a job. But what was the point of having such a beautiful home if it was just going to sit empty all day? She talked it over with William and they decided it was time to start a family.

A year later, after an easy pregnancy without morning sickness, heartburn, or hemorrhoids, Grace gave birth to their first child, a boy. They named him Charles. Grace had never known such pure happiness as that which she felt when rocking Charles in her arms and holding him to her milk-filled breasts.

The care and feeding of little Charles consumed her days, and often her nights as well. Grace seldom had time anymore to stare at herself in the mirror, but if she had, she would have seen that her

beautiful face looked tired now, puffy around the eyes, pale in the cheeks, a little drawn at the mouth. If William noticed these changes in his beautiful bride, he wisely made no comment except to say he liked the way she was wearing her hair these days, longer and loose. The truth was Grace had no time to wash and style it every morning like she used to, no time to go to the hairdresser for her monthly trim.

Grace was a careful new mother. When she wasn't tending to Charles, she was reading books about infant care and development and

how to increase your child's self-esteem. She often read these books late into the night with the bedside lamp glowing warmly beside her and the baby nestled in her arms. Charles was not a good sleeper and Grace could not bear to let him cry alone in his crib. So she often brought him into their bed and tucked him in beside her, which many of the parenting books said was the only healthy thing to do. Then William, who had to get up for work in the morning, would take some extra blankets and go and sleep on the couch. He said he didn't mind. He said he knew their lives would get back to normal again someday soon.

Little Charles thrived and grew strong and soon he was a healthy lively toddler. Grace wondered where the time had gone. Charles was walking, talking, and getting into mischief just like a two-year-old was supposed to. Much as Grace adored him, she missed having a little baby to snuggle. She talked it over with William and soon she was pregnant again. After another easy pregnancy, she gave birth to their second child, a girl this time. They named her Sarah.

Again Grace found herself looking tired and drawn, knee-deep in diapers, breast milk, and parenting books. Looking after two small children proved to be much harder than looking after one. They fussed and whined and drove her crazy with demands all day long. But as soon as William came home from work, they were all sweetness and smiles, Sarah making cute baby gooing sounds and Charles trailing his father around like a puppy dog. Grace could not help but resent this. Were the children, she wondered, sucking the life out of her on purpose or did it just happen that way? She couldn't very well tell William how she felt. Charles and Sarah were the equal apples of their father's eye.

William, as well as being an excellent provider, was also a wonderful father. He was not one of those old-fashioned men who thought

looking after children was woman's work. He was a modern, sensitive, hands-on father who fed and bathed his children, read them stories, played peekaboo and patty-cake with genuine delight, and changed their dirty diapers without gagging.

On sunny Sunday afternoons William would put Sarah up on his shoulders, take Charles by the hand, and off they would go to the park. Often the neighbors' children tagged along too. Their fathers, they each told him, were too busy, too grouchy, or too tired to play with them. They all adored William and wished their own fathers were just like him.

At the park William and the children played long laughing games of catch, tag, and hide-and-go-seek. William never seemed to tire of pushing them on the swings, catching them at the bottom of the big

silver slide, or simply chasing them around while growling like a ferocious bug-eyed monster.

Back at home alone, Grace thought about all the things she could
be doing while they were gone: constructive, creative, grown-up things.
But usually she did the laundry, the dishes, or the vacuuming. Sometimes she talked on the phone to her mother. Most often she went upstairs to the cool empty bedroom and had a nap. When William and
the children tumbled back into the house, boisterous and smelling of
sunshine and trees, she had to drag herself up from the uneasy depths
of her afternoon dreams. And then, sometimes, just for a minute, she
could not remember who they were.

Although many of Grace's days at home with the children seemed
never-ending, paradoxically the years themselves passed quickly. Soon
both Charles and Sarah were in school. They were bright, well-
behaved children, popular with both their teachers and their peers.
Grace was very proud of them. William was still a wonderful father
who often helped the children with their homework and never missed a
school concert or parent-teacher interview. He was now a full partner
in his firm and his annual salary was impressive. They could afford to
buy whatever they wanted. Even around the house Grace wore designer
dresses in all the latest styles. She was back in the habit now of having
her hair done at least once a month. Sometimes she had a manicure and
a pedicure too. William often told her she was even more beautiful now
than she'd been when they first met. He said, "You're not getting older,
you're getting better." He still bought her flowers for no reason, also
perfume, jewelry, and other pretty trinkets, tokens of his undying es-
teem. They made love often and well. William was never unfaithful.

Their home continued to be a source of great pride. Whenever
Grace felt a little bored with it, she bought a new carpet, new dining

room chairs, new drapes, or new artwork for the walls. These acquisitions always made her happy for a while.

Now that the children were in school all day, there was really no reason for Grace to stay home but she did. She thought about getting

a job. She wanted to do *something* but she wasn't sure what. She knew William would be supportive whatever she decided to do. She kept meaning to make a decision but somehow the days just got away on her. There was still so much to do. The children needed to be driven to and from school, to the dentist, the doctor, dance class, piano lessons, swimming, ceramics, gymnastics, and to the houses of their many friends. She had many hobbies that kept her busy too: embroidery, gardening, reading, and dried flower arranging. At last she had both the time and the energy to prepare those fabulous meals she and

William had dreamed of so long ago. Besides, she was used to staying home. And secretly she was more than a little afraid of the big world that lay beyond the windows of her safe and comfortable home.

Everyone said they were the perfect family and indeed they were. Grace had everything that she had ever wanted. Grace had everything that *everyone* had ever wanted. Grace was lucky.

So why did she often feel so sad?

Grace grew more and more depressed. William grew more and more concerned. Although he tried very hard to understand why she was so unhappy, he could not. Being perfectly happy himself, he was mystified by her misery. He sent her more and more flowers to cheer her up. Almost every day now a new bouquet would arrive, until every room was filled with them. But still Grace was often crying when he came home from work. He bought her a dog so she wouldn't be alone all day. Butch was a good dog and the children loved him, but he wasn't the answer to Grace's problems. William put big new windows in the din-

ing room so Grace wouldn't feel so trapped. After that, when William came home from work, he often found her staring at her own reflection in the glass, dinner not made and her hair not combed. He encouraged her to buy more designer dresses, more chairs, a new linen tablecloth, the antique tea set she'd had her eye on for months. Shopping had always made her happy before.

But nothing helped. Sensitive, supportive, and kind as he was, William once made the mistake of pointing out to Grace how lucky she was. This caused her to refuse to speak to him for three whole days. After that, William had to admit there was nothing he could do for her except hold her pretty hand and make sympathetic sounds in the back of his throat while she wept. He tried to be patient and to keep believing that their lives would get back to normal someday soon.

Obviously Grace needed someone else to talk to. She didn't like to burden her mother with her problems because her mother and father were so proud of her, so happy for her. She could not now admit to them that she was unhappy. They would be so disappointed. She could not let them down. Whenever Grace talked to her parents, she said, "Everything is wonderful, just wonderful!" And of course they believed her.

Grace began tracking down and calling up some of her old friends. These were the women who had been secretly envious of her in the early years, the women she had lost touch with when her children were small and she was too busy and too tired to have friends. These were the women whose lives, she imagined, had turned out much like her own.

But when Grace told these women her troubles, they were not nearly as understanding as she had expected.

The first woman said, "You think *you've* got problems! I've got varicose veins, chronic back pain, and hemorrhoids. My husband goes out and gets drunk every night and my daughter has green hair and three rings in her nose."

The second woman said, "What are *you* complaining about? I'm thirty pounds overweight, my thighs are the size of tree stumps, and my husband is sleeping with my best friend. My son was caught smoking dope at recess and my daughter worships Satan. I've got to go now, I'm getting a migraine."

The third woman said, "You don't know how lucky you are! My husband lost his job and I'm flipping burgers to make ends meet. I've got bunions, an ulcer, and my breasts are shrinking. My son just poisoned the cat and my daughter won't eat meat."

The fourth woman said, "Cry me a river! What right have *you* got to be unhappy? My husband left me for a younger woman and my lover went back to his wife. My children are in therapy and my hair is falling out because of all this stress."

Some of these women offered advice. "Have another baby," they said. "Have a face lift. Have a tummy tuck. Have an affair. Have your cake and eat it too!"

"Count your blessings!" they all cried. "Count your blessings and be quiet!"

So she did. She counted her blessings like sheep, night after insomniac night while William snored on beside her.

These were the women who meant to be warriors. These were the women who had fully intended to take the world by storm. They had thrown off their shackles and donned the adamant armor of the women's movement. They had wielded the weapons of intelligence and equal rights in one hand, while still brandishing the blessings of beauty and femininity in the other. These were the women who believed they could have it all. They had every reason to expect that, after all the battles they had won and all the strides they had taken, they would ultimately spread their wings and be free.

These were the women who had imagined they would always be true to themselves, would follow their hearts *and* their heads, would never succumb to bourgeois conventionality or be held in bondage by the power of men. They intended to speak out loudly and proudly, proclaiming their own stories for all the world to see. They intended to live lives of adventure, accomplishment, and the complete satisfaction of their every desire.

These were the women who said they would never worry about aging, who intended to wear their wrinkles with pride, who would never dye their hair. They would become wise old women, powerful

lusty crones, respected and revered, the sage and sovereign swans of the postmodern world. And when the time came, their swan songs would be exquisite.

See what has become of them. Look at them, just look at them now. Imagine their surprise, their disappointment, at having ended up here.

*   *   *

Grace thought long and hard about blessings and luck. She pondered the problems of women. Busy with her own perfect life, safe inside her own beautiful house for all these years, she had not fully grasped the extent of them, the magnitude, the range, the versatility, the sheer titanic number of ways a woman's life could go wrong.

No one had ever warned her that luck did not necessarily lead to happiness. No one had ever warned her to be careful what she wished for.

Now she could feel them, all the unhappy women waiting at the bottom of the stairs, clamoring at the gate, rattling their chains. She could hear their voices, screeching, strident, and shrill.

One by one they cried out to her:

"A faithful, intelligent, handsome husband who worships the ground you walk on!"

"Two healthy, clever, well-adjusted children who respect, admire, and love you with all their little hearts!"

"A flat stomach, flawless skin, straight teeth, long legs, breasts still perky, buttocks still firm, and not a single stretch mark in sight!"

"All the bills paid without worry, the mortgage payment made on time, and there's always more where that came from!"

"A life of leisure!"

"A beautiful home!"

"The dresses, the hats, the shoes of your dreams!"

"And it's not enough! It's just not enough!"

It was still not enough.

They beat their breasts and pulled out their hair. They banged their pretty heads against the pretty walls. They tore off their clothes till there were heaving bosoms and big brown nipples everywhere.

They marched by the thousands through the hot dark night, a stampede of unhappy women demanding to be heard. They flexed their little muscles and stamped their dainty feet. They ranted and raved, they bellowed and roared, they hollered and grumbled and howled. They whipped themselves into a frenzy until, eventually, exhausted, they quivered and stumbled and fell to the ground in a heap. They whimpered and sniveled and wept.

But no one heard them. No one listened. No one except Grace.

The problems of women, Grace realized now, were like a swarming plague of locusts let loose upon the land.

They had sagging breasts, baggy buttocks, double chins, and wrinkles. They had varicose veins, cellulite, stretch marks, and mustaches. They had chronic depression and low self-esteem. They had menstrual cramps, yeast infections, ovarian cysts, and vaginal itching. They had menopause.

They had unfaithful husbands, ungrateful children, and underpaid jobs. They had unsatisfied longings, unarticulated yearnings, frustrated ambitions, and thwarted desires. They had housework.

They had nothing to look forward to but more of the same.

By now Grace was so depressed, some mornings she couldn't even get out of bed. The children were so busy with their own lives that they hardly noticed. They did, however, stop inviting their friends over after school for fear of finding Grace still in bed or standing in her nightgown staring at herself in the dining room windows or the full-length mirror, her hair all matted and a half-eaten box of doughnuts in her hand.

William carefully suggested that perhaps it was time for professional help. He arranged an appointment with a doctor reputed to be the very best in the field of female problems. Because Grace was so incapacitated, this doctor generously agreed to make a house call.

First he coaxed Grace out of bed and then he proceeded to examine her. He was thorough and kind. He shone a little light into her eyes and then into her ears. He tested her reflexes which were sluggish and took her pulse which was slow. He slipped his cold stethoscope inside her nightgown and listened to her heart both front and back. He patted her hand which was limp and checked her blood pressure which was low. He asked if she had headaches, double vision, nausea, flatulence, or tingling in her fingers and toes. He asked after the condition of her reproductive organs which were fine and after her state of mind which, obviously, was not.

When he was finished, he smiled sympathetically and nodded his wise head. He pointed at her with one long finger and said, "You, my dear, are in terrible shape!" Grace already knew this.

"Can you help me?" she whispered desperately.

"Of course I can," he answered heartily. "Of course I can help you, but your case calls for drastic measures." He turned to look at the clock on the wall. "Come now, come now, there's no time to waste!"

The doctor led Grace down the stairs and into her beautiful kitchen. Grace did not question him. He was a doctor. She trusted him.

He asked her to take off her clothes. She did.

He asked her to lie down on the table. She did. The white linen tablecloth was clean and soft beneath her naked back.

He touched her elegant neck and her graceful shoulders. He patted her long auburn hair which hung over the edge of the table. He admired her generous but not floppy breasts and her shapely but not heavy hips. He complimented her on her flat stomach and her tasteful navel.

He covered her long legs and her dainty little feet with the end of the tablecloth and then placed a white dish towel on her chest.

He opened his medical bag and took out a needle. The prick in her arm was so small she hardly felt it.

As Grace began to fall asleep, the kitchen filled with streaming beams of sunlight and pearly pillowy clouds. Angels gathered, the spirits of women, would-be warriors, itinerant swans. Music played, a rousing march of ascension interspersed with female voices, chanting.

The doctor held a knife in his hand.

He leaned over Grace, smiling sympathetically and nodding his wise head.

He made one careful cut to her left breast.

Another cut.

Another.

There was no blood. There was no pain.

And then he ripped her heart out.

RULES OF THUMB:
AN ALPHABET OF
IMPERATIVES FOR
THE MODERN AGE

void the temptations of envy, pride, fast food, and daytime TV talk shows. Succumbing to the temptation of envy will turn you into a bitter and twisted person who is unable to share in the happy love affairs and dazzling career triumphs of your friends. When they call you all excited to tell you how wonderful their lives are, you will change the subject. Soon they will stop calling and you will end up not only bitter and twisted, but very lonely as well. You will have to go for lunch all by yourself.

If, on the other hand, you succumb to the temptation of pride and go around telling everyone about your many career accomplishments and your amazing sex life, you too will end up having lunch alone. (Despite all those self-help books touting the importance of high self-esteem, most people, when faced with it in real life, find it very annoying. Most people prefer to hang around with others whose self-esteem is as low as their own.)

One obvious antidote to both envy and pride is gossip. If you know a secret about one of your former friends, you are honor-bound to tell it to the rest of the group. They, of course, must be sworn to secrecy before they can then go ahead and spread the nasty rumor around. Remember that gossip is no good without names, dates, and graphic details. Remember that everything you say can and will be used against you once it finds its way back, as it always does, to the person whose beans you spilled.

The end result of all this envy, pride, and gossip will be a number of upscale downtown restaurants filled each day at noon with well-dressed people having lunch at pretty little tables for one. They all read while they eat so as to avoid having to meet the eyes of the other solitary diners.

At this uncomfortable juncture, you may find yourself fleeing to the fast food outlet across the street where you can indulge in a greasy double cheeseburger and a Styrofoam bucket of fries and gravy without running the risk of seeing anyone you know. It is here (and only here) that you may safely engage in an animated conversation with a total stranger at the next table about the talk show you saw on Monday afternoon when you left work early and the topic was "My Mother Is Having My Boyfriend's Baby." It is here (and only here) on your orange plastic chair at your white plastic table, eating off your brown plastic tray, that you may safely admit that you love these shows because they prove that the world is full of losers whose lives are much more miserable than your own.

e ironic whenever possible. In this age of anxiety a sense of humor may be your most valuable asset. Learn to spot ironic opportunities everywhere. Make sarcastic comments about anything commonly held dear to most (less clever) people's hearts. Conversations not filled with witty repartee and self-congratulatory laughter are seldom worth having. Never be naive or sentimental unless you can do so in an ironic way. If you take pleasure in certain pastimes which are no longer considered chic, be sure to do so ironically. If, for instance, you belong to a weekend bowling league, buy your own two-toned bowling shoes and a turquoise marblized bowling ball with a monogrammed vinyl carrying bag.

To become a true master of irony, you must learn to be ironic without even opening your mouth. Adopt an ironic smile, an ironic wardrobe, an ironic (but not unflattering) hairstyle, and, above all, an ironic posture which will enable you to lounge ironically against any available vertical surface while sipping an ironic glass of Perrier water or imported draft beer.

After yet another evening spent smiling and slouching while occasionally flinging about clever insults and aphorisms, you may wind up at home alone feeling a little ashamed of yourself, a little dirty perhaps, a little less than genuine. It is safe to disregard these niggling misgivings because, after a good night's sleep, you will wake up feeling refreshed and ironic all over again. This is the beauty of irony: once you've got the hang of it, you'll never have to take yourself seriously again.

(A word of caution: There are still some behaviors and pastimes which can never be categorized as ironic. These include: committing any type of violent and/or sexual crime, displaying racist lawn ornaments in your front yard, wearing a mink coat, collecting stamps, owls, or unicorns, reading pornographic magazines, vomiting in someone else's car, and sleeping with your best friend's spouse.)

 onsider yourself lucky if you have a satisfying career, a loving partner, or a well-insulated (and tastefully decorated) roof over your head. If you have all three of these, consider yourself miraculous. Try not to dwell on the fact that your perfect life is probably too good to be true and so is more than likely to fall apart any minute now. Try not to be overcome too often by a sense of impending doom.

If you find that you must associate (through no fault of your own) with people whose lives are generally a mess, try not to be smug. Try to be sympathetic and encouraging. Assure them repeatedly that someday their ship too will come in. In the meantime hang on fiercely to all that you have got and do not lend them money, your trench coat, or your car. (Sharing is a noble concept which should be instilled in all small children but is advisable to grow out of once you become a successful adult.) If these hapless people annoyingly persist in harping on how lucky you are, point out to them that it was not luck, it was just good planning on your part. Assure them repeatedly that life is what you make it and that, in the end, everybody gets what they deserve.

evelop a taste for foreign food. This does not mean pizza, spaghetti, egg rolls, fortune cookies, French fries, or French toast. This means elaborate unusual dishes with unpronounceable names featuring many exotic (and expensive) ingredients available only in specialty stores (or, in extreme cases, by mail order). Purchasing these ingredients will necessitate running all over town, popping in and out of small fragrant stores all day long with your recipe clutched in your hand. Although this may be rather time-consuming, you will be spared the unfortunate experience of shopping in a large supermarket where you would be forced, under unflattering fluorescent lighting, to rub carts with all manner of uninteresting people intent on accumulating a whole week's supply of wieners, Wonder bread, canned peas, Cheez Whiz, and Hamburger Helper (with which they will then feed their many children who are now riding around in their shopping carts while screaming at the top of their lungs and throwing jars of Miracle Whip on the floor).

By perfecting your eclectic meal-by-meal marketing technique, you will eventually find it necessary to venture into a supermarket only occasionally, to purchase such unamusing and yet useful staples as floor wax, laundry detergent, dish soap, and toilet paper.

(Please note: If, in times of stress or laziness, you still harbor a residual fondness for certain foods available only in supermarkets—

items such as butterscotch pudding, frozen waffles, Spam, or Froot Loops—remember that these should be consumed only in the privacy of your own home, preferably late at night while watching television in your flannelette pajamas and your bunny slippers. Such deviant indulgences are acceptable only if you refer to them as *comfort food* and nobody else ever sees you eating them.)

xhibit a marked sartorial preference for the color black, especially if you are involved (even marginally) in pursuits of an artistic or literary nature. Whatever the occasion, black is always not only acceptable but positively preferable.

When shopping for clothes, you will be pleased to discover that there is apparently no limit to the variations available within this color scheme. Black clothes, you will observe, are like snowflakes: no two of them exactly alike. You should acquire as many versions as possible of: the little black dress, the little black suit, the little black shirt, the little black sweater, the little black skirt, and the little black pair of pants.

As far as accessories are concerned, you will want to accumulate a comprehensive selection of black belts, black gloves, black stockings, black scarves, and black shoes. (Black underwear remains a matter of personal preference and is, you should realize, often misunderstood.) A black leather jacket, no longer worn only to accessorize a motorcycle, is now considered tasteful across all social strata.

The versatility of black clothing knows no bounds. Not only does an all-black wardrobe elevate the notion of mix-and-match to a fine art, it also bears no seasonal restrictions. Although it is still considered *déclassé* to wear white after Labor Day, black is as welcome at a picnic as at a Christmas party.

If on occasion you feel the urge to break out of this monochromatism you may introduce (with discretion and restraint) items of the following colors: white, off-white, eggshell, ivory, ecru, beige, tan, ocher, and oyster. Under no circumstances whatsoever is it permissible to include anything in lime green, hot pink, or fluorescent orange. Indeed, if the store in which you are shopping does sell clothing in any of these colors, you are in the wrong place and should evacuate the premises immediately.

ind yourself a good therapist whether you think you need one or not. Chances are that if you don't need one right now, sooner or later (probably sooner) you will. The choice of a therapist is a complicated process in which you must give lengthy consideration to the age, gender, wardrobe, sexual orientation, and educational credentials of each candidate. Do not neglect to also evaluate the issues of office location and decor. Do your research thoroughly to gather a clear picture of each candidate's success rate with other clients. If, for example, the most maladjusted insane person you know has been seeing the same therapist twice a week for the past twenty years with no signs of progress, do not go there. Also be wary of any therapist who sees your spouse, your ex-spouse, your lover, your other lover, your best friend, your boss, or your cleaning lady.

The advantage to engaging a therapist well in advance of a crisis is that by the time you do fall apart completely, you and your therapist will have already made your way through the emotional scars incurred between the ages of three and twelve, the soul-destroying humiliation of adolescence, the substance abuse of early adulthood, and the volcanic eruption of your first marriage. These issues having been resolved, you will now be able to tend, without further ado, to the nervous breakdown at hand.

loss over any past incidents or indiscretions which do not show you in your best light. There is no need to ever mention, for instance, the weekend you went bar-hopping with a motorcycle gang, the year you were flat broke and developed a taste for Kraft Dinner and fried baloney, or the time you got drunk at a party and spent the night with a short-order cook whose name you couldn't remember in the morning. Save such unflattering reminiscences for your therapist.

Any notion that a bout of true confessions will be perceived by others as endearing and that they will like you more for your unflinching honesty is completely false. The truth is nothing can possibly be accomplished by making yourself look bad and the people to whom you have confessed such episodes will never let you live them down.

Rather, adopt a revisionist stance toward your own history. Your goal should be to make everybody believe that you have always been as virtuous, sophisticated, and affluent as you are now.

ave an opinion on everything. Give the distinct impression that nothing in the modern world has escaped your notice. Exhibit the astounding range of your knowledge as often as possible. This knowledge should encompass all subject areas. You should, for instance, be well-versed in politics at the world level. (Familiarity with municipal politics is optional, not mandatory.) You must keep abreast of both national and global current events. Be sure though that you are never perceived to be actually *studying* such issues. You are much too busy for that. People will marvel at how well-informed you are and conclude that you must have acquired such a wealth of information by osmosis.

You should be an expert on all forms of art, music, theater, dance, and literature. Have an opinion on all contemporary books whether you have actually read them or not. The same goes for movies, both foreign and domestic, which you must always refer to as *films.* It is to your advantage to also have an opinion on all recent medical and dietary innovations, all technological advances, weather patterns, fashion trends, and high-profile murder trials.

Do not be shy about expressing said opinions on everything. Do so with complete certainty and unshakable equanimity. Do so in an assertive and confident manner which makes all dissenting opinions look ridiculous. (Do not withhold judgment for any reason. Do not suffer fools gladly.)

If ever you do find yourself in the distressing situation of being without an opinion, agree repeatedly with the opinion which sounds closest to the opinion you would have if you had one. Register this agreement by repeatedly exclaiming with profound enthusiasm, "Absolutely!"

mply that if you were in charge, the world would be a much kinder, cleaner, more civilized place: a place long since made free of rap music, panhandlers, vacuum cleaner salesmen, telemarketers, rude parking lot attendants, velvet paintings, romance novels, plastic cutlery, Styrofoam coffee cups, frozen pizza, and all desserts featuring colored marshmallows and shredded coconut. Indicate that, upon the eventual assumption of your rightful position as worldwide arbiter of good taste, you will immediately implement a policy of zero tolerance for polyester, spandex, crushed velvet, orange satin bedspreads, and leopardskin stretchies.

oin a variety of clubs and/or service organizations at which you are likely to meet people even more interesting and influential than the people you already know. Having joined the downtown fitness club, for instance, you may one day find yourself on the rowing machine next to the man who owns the most prestigious art gallery in town. In the event of such a fortuitous encounter, you must be able to initiate and conduct an intelligent critical discussion of surrealism without grunting, moaning, or dripping sweat in this man's general direction.

The decision of which club to grace with your presence must be considered very carefully. Do not join a singles club unless you are indeed single. Do not join any group that holds séances during which the members attempt to contact the spirits of their dead relatives with a Ouija board. Do not join any club whose members are required to perform a secret handshake and wear unattractive uniforms (such as white sheets or shiny red suits with funny tasseled hats). Do not join any organization which refers to its place of meeting as "the clubhouse." In such a case, you have blundered into either a preschool play group or a motorcycle gang.

(Please note: If you decide to join a club which involves any athletic activity, be it downhill skiing, synchronized swimming, lawn bowling, badminton, tennis, or darts, be sure that you are already proficient in this activity so as to avoid incurring serious injury or embarrassing yourself in front of a bunch of total strangers.)

now that other people may not find your children as charming as you do. Even those people who apparently dote upon their own children to the point of distraction may not dote similarly upon yours. Be aware that, although many traditional notions have fallen by the wayside over the years, the old adage that children should be seen and not heard remains as true today as it ever was. Indeed you may now expand this good advice to include the codicil that children should not be seen too often or heard about too much.

Remember that small children are seldom welcome at fine restaurants, poetry readings, or the opera. (They are also not popular on airplanes but sometimes their presence in such a situation is unavoidable.) Remember that small children are most enjoyable to others when they are at home asleep under the watchful care of a reliable babysitter.

Securing the services of said babysitter is an important subject not usually covered in prenatal classes but it should be. Arrangements for such supplementary child care should be made well in advance of the birth itself. Even before you begin decorating the nursery, you should be compiling an extensive list of people who will be available at a moment's notice for the next thirteen years or so. The most desirable babysitters are adults who have no social lives of their own. Not only are they likely to be more responsible, but they won't have to be home by ten o'clock when the party you're going to doesn't start until nine-thirty.

(A small but important point: It is still considered good parenting practice to carry photographs of your children in your wallet at all times. However, when showing these around at a business luncheon or a fancy dinner party, remember that the maximum of two photographs per child must be strictly observed.)

eave the contemplation of the question "What is the meaning of life?" to others whose temperaments make them more naturally suited to the task: that is to say, philosophers, poets, Tibetan monks, and other depressive types who inhabit the fringes of modern society.

This question invariably leads, by some process of metaphysical mutation, to more questions like: "Who am I really? Why am I here? Is there life after death? Who invented plastic rain hats? Why do we want blue toilet water?" Prolonged speculation in these areas will lead you to the conclusion that such questions have no answers. This in turn will lead to a migraine headache and the suspicion that life may not be worth living after all.

Remember that, although a sense of style, a full passport, and an Armani suit may not make your life more meaningful, they will definitely make it more satisfying. Just as it is not necessary to understand the workings of the internal combustion engine in order to drive your silver Lexus, similarly, understanding the meaning of life is not a prerequisite to living well. Remember that a new silver Lexus with a genuine leather and wood interior operates on the same principle as an old yellow Honda Civic with no muffler. Which would you rather drive? Now there is a question that bears asking.

(A helpful hint: If you do occasionally find that this meaning-of-life issue insists upon rearing its ugly head despite your best efforts to ignore it, it is best to discuss it with, and only with, your therapist. Such topics do not, generally speaking, make for scintillating dinner conversation and your social life will suffer accordingly. Your therapist, however, may be able to shed some light on this particular conundrum and will be happy to introduce you to such terms as *existentialism, midlife crisis,* and *clinically depressed.*)

aster many useful and unusual skills in your spare time. The possibilities here are endless. For starters, you should learn how to blow glass, raise peacocks, play water polo, build a log cabin, mix concrete, make lace, milk a cow, play the clarinet, fly a small plane, make paper, spin wool, change a car engine, grow orchids, make pretzels, and carve duck decoys. (Of course you are already an expert at baking, sewing, weaving, goldsmithing, computer programming, and underwater photography.)

The more skills you master, the more people will admire you to your face and call you nasty names behind your back. Be patient with them. They are just jealous. Suggest that they too might benefit immeasurably from an evening course in origami, upholstery, or the history of art. Unless of course they would prefer that you tutor them yourself.

ever wear earrings shaped like cats, dogs, horses, pumpkins, turkeys, palm trees, or Santa Claus.

Never use cheap shampoo.

Never serve pretzels as an hors d'oeuvre. (Unless of course you made them yourself.)

Never wear sweatpants (not even your black ones) in public.

Never wear socks with sandals or white sneakers with a business suit.

Never pay cash for a restaurant meal. Always use your gold card.

Never drink beer (or wine, for that matter) straight from the bottle.

Never comb your hair, pick your teeth, blow your nose, or scratch anywhere below the shoulders in front of other people.

Never confess that you once bought a pair of shoes at Wal-Mart.

Never admit that you don't like eggplant, even when it's called *aubergine.*

Never admit that you were wrong. (Mistaken, maybe, but never just plain wrong.)

ffer advice freely. Although your friends and acquaintances may not, at first glance, appear to be asking for your advice, in truth, they always need it. Although they may insist that all they want is someone to *listen* to their problems, in truth, what they really want is someone to *solve* them.

The prime area of modern life which most consistently and desperately begs for advice is, of course, the romantic relationship. Assuming that you have a perfect relationship (complete with honesty, respect, great sex, and a fifty-fifty split on all household duties and expenses), what better person could there possibly be to assume the all-important responsibility of telling others how to run their love lives?

Such advice is best dispensed in small intimate groups of two or three people gathered together over a tasty garlic-laden lunch followed by many cups of fresh-ground coffee and/or many glasses of good white wine. Under such genial circumstances, almost anyone will feel free to spill his or her guts. Listen politely while nodding wisely, smiling warmly, and patting hands as required. Once the current problem has been sufficiently aired and you have assessed the gravity of the situation, then it is your turn to talk. Begin with the sentence, "Well . . . *I* know what *I* would do if *I* were you." Proceed to explain exactly what you would do which is also exactly what he or she should do. Although he or she may initially be resentful of or resistant to your suggestion of an affair, a divorce, or celibacy for a year or two, eventually he or she will thank you for it—even if, in the meantime, he or she stops speaking to you and frequently crosses busy streets to avoid running into you.

(A word of advice to advanced advice-givers: Do not feel obliged to restrict yourself to advice of a romantic nature. Branch out and offer guidance on a diverse range of topics including home improvement, interior decorating, career and parenting strategies, medical treatment, organic gardening, Vietnamese cooking, aerobic exercise, and the best brand of breath mints.)

repare extensively prior to attendance at any significant social event. First, get a copy of the guest list so you know who else will be there. Determine as fully as possible who of these people is currently not speaking to you and who among them are not speaking to each other.

Assess the volatility of these various rifts so as to be alert to the possible eruption of unseemly shouting matches and/or fistfights. Forewarned is, as they say, forearmed. Bearing all this in mind in advance will prepare you for the diffusion of any uncomfortable encounters and will serve as a useful reminder as to whom you may safely insult in front of whom. If you anticipate an unavoidable confrontation of any kind, rehearse your speech beforehand. There is nothing worse than being caught unprepared by someone who has been leaving unpleasant messages on your answering machine for the last two weeks.

If possible, also find out who will be wearing what so as to avoid any unintentional and embarrassing duplication of fashion statements.

If there appear on the guest list any important people with whom you are not yet acquainted, find out the respective specialties of said people and do some research. If among the guests there will be a microbiologist, a theoretical physicist, a paleontologist, a world-renowned neurosurgeon, and a sound poet, acquire at least a basic knowledge of each of these subject areas which you may then exhibit at your leisure throughout the evening. Leave the distinct impression that you are an authority on everything. (Rest assured that, no matter what anybody says, this is not the same thing as being a know-it-all.)

uit smoking, drinking to excess, and listening to loud rock-and-roll music. Smoking is no longer an acceptable bad habit. If you do persist, you will observe that it is becoming increasingly difficult to find a place where smoking is still permitted. Most of these remaining places are out-of-doors.

Consequently, as an inveterate smoker, you will find yourself repeatedly huddled with a bunch of other smokers on porches, patios, balconies, park benches, in back alleys, parking lots, and the doorways of office buildings, fancy restaurants, and four-star hotels. Nine times out of ten it will be raining, snowing, or thirty below. This practice will cause you to bond with all manner of people to whom you would not give the time of day under ordinary circumstances.

Similarly, drinking to excess is no longer considered charming (not even in those artistic and literary circles formerly renowned for their alcohol consumption). It is no longer an admirable accomplishment to be able to drink all your friends under the table. Now you should confine yourself, on any given evening, to one or two glasses of wine and then you should switch to coffee. Drinking large amounts of coffee late at night will cause you to feel every bit as hungover in the morning as if you had single-handedly polished off two bottles of wine the night before. But you will not be faced with that humiliating task of having to call everyone and ask them what you did last night. Even better than drinking in moderation is abstaining altogether. While remaining perfectly sober yourself, you will be vastly entertained by watching all your friends become stupider and stupider as the evening wears on.

Listening to loud rock-and-roll music is a pastime which should be engaged in only by angst-ridden adolescents. Having reached a certain age, you should be listening exclusively to classical music, opera, jazz, and/or whale songs. An occasional bout with the Rolling Stones is acceptable, but only for nostalgic purposes. Other than that, any music to which you can dance, sing along, or cry your eyes out is nothing more than juvenile and should be avoided at all costs.

adiate at all times an aura of self-confidence, self-reliance, and self-control. Emit an air of refinement, maturity, and sophistication like a hundred-dollar-an-ounce perfume. Suppress the urge ever to admit to anyone that sometimes you feel inadequate, inferior, insecure, insignificant, and easily intimidated (by your boss, your children's friends, and/or your hairdresser). Never confess to feeling anxious, clumsy, unattractive, unappreciated, unhappy, or very vulnerable. It is not to your advantage to admit that you too are afraid of dying and are well aware of the fact that all the confidence and good taste in the world will not make you immortal. Especially never admit (not even to your best friend) that sometimes you feel all day long like crying for no good reason and that sometimes you do just that. There is nothing worse than having somebody feel sorry for you.

pare no effort or expense when it comes to furnishing and decorating your home. Although you may be too busy to spend much time there, still, your home is your castle and must be outfitted accordingly. Settle for nothing but the best. In interior decoration (as in many other important areas), it is easier to know what you *don't* want than what you *do.* Steer clear of any home decorating style that contains the word *modern* and involves vinyl, plaid, shag carpeting, lava lamps, vertical blinds, and the colors orange, purple, and/or avocado. Never purchase any item that says on the box, *Looks just like real wood* or

Some assembly required. Avoid anything described as *faux* because, obviously, it is likely to be only a hop, skip, and a jump away from *faux pas.*

There are many commandments which must be obeyed in this area. The three most important of these are to err always on the side of the traditional, to keep your home immaculate at all times, and never to put your television in the living room.

urn against all those who have ever contradicted you in public, failed to laugh at your witty repartee, questioned your right to suggest they should seek professional help, criticized your spouse (your child, your wardrobe, your hair color, your antipasto, or your grasp of experimental theater). Bear a grudge against these people forever. Especially bear a grudge against anyone who has ever told you that you looked tired when you weren't.

While secretly indulging in elaborate revenge fantasies in which these people are dramatically humiliated for once and for all, in public express these grudges in a civilized manner. Forget to invite these people to your summer solstice party. Forget to call them on their birthdays. Take their numbers off your programmable phone. Do not return their calls. Tell them your answering machine is broken. Lose the umbrella, the book, the Bundt pan, the kid leather gloves that you borrowed.

When encountering these people in public, do not embrace them and kiss them on both cheeks the way you do with your *real* friends. Tell them you didn't see them downtown last Saturday afternoon when you were going into the Chinese grocery and they were just coming out. If any of these people are childish enough to ask if you're avoiding them, say incredulously, "Of course not! Why would I do such a thing? You know me better than that!"

nderstand that the average suburban shopping mall was intended for a class of people to which you do not belong. Such places should be frequented only as a last resort. They may, for instance, be useful in November when you are just finishing up your Christmas shopping. (You, needless to say, are not the kind of person who leaves this task to the very last minute.) There may be, through no fault of your own, a handful of people on your extensive Christmas list (relatives, employees, neighbors, and the like) whose tastes run toward the sort of merchandise carried only in malls.

If you have small children, you may find yourself forced to visit the mall on a rainy Saturday afternoon when they cannot possibly be taken to the park instead. (Having become a parent, you will frequently find yourself doing things that formerly you wouldn't have been caught dead at. This includes having hamburgers or pizza in the food court at the mall while surrounded by other families desperate for something to do and by mangy adolescents and adults who apparently do this because they like it.) After an hour or two of being dragged around the overheated mall with their winter coats hanging off them, your children will be more than ready to go home and have a nap.

Milling through a crowded, noisy, often malodorous shopping mall cannot possibly be good for your image or your morale. Many trips to the mall end up with everyone crying in the car in the parking lot.

Strive to be the kind of person no one can ever imagine trudging through the mall with a cart full of plastic place mats, vacuum cleaner bags, a stuffed purple dinosaur, a toilet brush, a Weed Eater, a hamster cage, and a twenty-pound bag of kitty litter.

alue your time and organize it wisely. What with all the things you have to do, all the places you have to go, and all the people you have to see, your time is at a premium. Assuming that, in addition to all of these pursuits, you must also devote a certain number of hours to a job each day, efficient time management is all the more crucial. Implement a variety of tools and techniques toward this end. Most important of these is the leather-bound gold-embossed appointment book. (A zippered closure is a discretionary but always impressive option.) Be sure to select a book which features a whole page per day. Your busy life cannot possibly be contained within a two-inch-square block of white space.

Recent technological developments have made time management even more complex and time-consuming. You may wish to take advantage of these advances by purchasing a pocket-size electronic organizer for each family member and/or by installing on your home computer a calendar program complete for the next fifteen years. This will allow you to see the future in reassuring detail. If you have already noted several important social commitments in the year 2003, you need no longer be plagued by the suspicion that nobody likes you and that you are being left out of all kinds of interesting things. Even more importantly, a calendar filled years in advance will effectively ward off those feelings of emptiness and ennui which invariably lead to the contemplation of that pesky meaning-of-life issue.

(A word of comfort: If, upon catching a glimpse of your intricate time management system, your friends begin to bandy about such phrases as *anal retentive* and *control freak*, feel free to smugly ignore them. Take consolation in the knowledge that three months from now when you are having the time of your life at a fund-raising dinner for animal rights, they will be at home alone washing their hair because they thought the dinner was next week.)

elcome any opportunity to improve and expand your vocabulary. Learn the proper spelling, meaning, and usage of such words as: *semiotics, solipsism, obsequious, oligarchy, palimpsest, epistemology, fiduciary,* and *polytetrafluoroethylene.* Any conversation will be elevated and enlivened by the timely insertion of these and other polysyllabic terms. Never miss an opportunity to use the words *dysfunctional, empowerment, Tuscany,* and *radiccio.* Whenever possible, use them all in one sentence.

enophilia: cultivate it. (If you have not yet improved your vocabulary, the word *xenophilia* refers to "a mania for, obsession with, or inordinate attraction to foreigners and all things foreign.") Cultivate a love for all things imported, including wine, food, clothing, cars, carpets, and films. Subscribe to the belief that anything of domestic origin is inherently inferior to its foreign counterpart.

Especially cultivate an interest in geography. Even if you have neither the means nor the inclination to travel, stock up on guidebooks to all the best countries. This will enable you to participate effectively in those sophisticated dinner conversations in which all the other guests discuss their most recent vacations abroad.

On their vacations, these people do not go to Bemidji, Minnesota, for the last two weeks of July. They also do not go to Disneyland, to Niagara Falls, or to Winnipeg to visit their elderly aunt. These people go to the Greek islands, the Black Forest, Tuscany, Costa del Sol, Istanbul, and Paris.

Having studied your guidebooks, you too will know that the best rooms at the Grand Hotel Summer Palace in Rhodes are situated in the new wing, featuring pink marble floors and marvelous paintings of water nymphs and goddesses. That at Tuscany's Museo dell'Opera del Duomo (formerly the bishop's palace) you can view Donatello's original reliefs for the Pulpit of the Holy Girdle (admission 5,000 lire, closed on Tuesday). That at Les Bookinistes on the Left Bank (fifth bistro annex of chef Guy Savoy, a charming postmodern room with a delightful view of the Seine) the mussel and pumpkin soup is the perfect appetizer to precede the ravioli stuffed with chicken and celery (closed on Sunday, no lunch Saturday).

Refrain at these gatherings from putting forth your theory that people who travel excessively are usually running away from their real lives at home.

Also do not mention your recurring nightmare in which you, having finally made your way to Paris, stroll into a charming *brasserie* in *l'arrondissement seizième* only to find all of them assembled there *pour le déjeuner.*

When in the company of these urbane frequent-flyers, avoid the word *pretentious.*

earn in public for the good old days when life was simpler, the air was cleaner, and the food was fresher. In private, get down on your knees and thank the Lord for the cellphone, the laptop, the fax, the modem, the microwave, the electric bread maker, the self-defrosting freezer, the automatic teller machine, the remote control car starter, voice mail, and antibiotics.

Especially thank the Lord for your electronic sound machine which allows you to listen to the ocean, the gentle patter of rain, the babbling of a brook, or the relaxing lullaby of a summer night (complete with crickets and frogs) whenever you need to escape from the unrelenting stress of modern life. The added beauty of this machine is that it allows you to commune with nature without actually having to go outside where you would run the risk of getting wet and dirty, not to mention the possibility of being bitten by mosquitoes, black-flies, or a rabid raccoon.

ealously embrace the pursuit of perfection. Simple self-improvement is no longer enough. Strive at all times to ascend to the absolute zenith of style and so-phistication. No matter how self-satisfied you may be at any given moment, remember that there is always more work to be done. Take heart. Take pride. Take the bull by the horns. Take over. Take credit. Take charge. Take notes when necessary.

Above all else, take strength from the knowledge that the cream always rises to the top.

SOURCES FOR ILLUSTRATIONS

Some of the illustrations in this book appear in their original form. Others are collages created by the author.

The illustrations were taken from *Images of Medicine: A Definitive Volume of More than 4,800 Copyright-free Engravings,* edited by Jim Harter (Bonanza Books, New York, 1991) and from the following volumes of the Dover Pictorial Archive Series (Dover Publications, New York):

200 Decorative Title-Pages (Alexander Nesbitt); *3800 Early Advertising Cuts* (Carol Belanger Grafton); *Albinus on Anatomy* (Robert Beverly Hale and Terence Coyle); *Animals* (Jim Harter); *Cesare Ripa: Baroque and Rococo Pictorial Imagery* (Edward A. Maser); *Children* (Carol Belanger Grafton); *Decorative Alphabets and Initials* (Alexander Nesbitt); *A Diderot Pictorial Encyclopedia of Trades and Industry: Volumes One and Two* (Charles C. Gillispie); *The Doré Bible Illustrations* (Millicent Rose); *Early American Locomotives* (John H. White, Jr.); *Food and Drink* (Jim Harter); *Goods and Merchandise* (William Rowe); *Handbook of Renaissance Ornament* (Albert Fidelis Butsch); *Harter's Picture Archive for Collage and Illustration* (Jim Harter); *Historic Alphabets and Initials* (Carol Belanger Grafton); *Love and Romance* (Carol Belanger Grafton); *Men* (Jim Harter); *Montgomery Ward & Co. Catalogue and Buyers' Guide, No. 57, Spring and Summer 1895* (Boris Emmet); *Music* (Jim Harter); *The New Testament* (Don Rice); *Old-Fashioned Animal Cuts* (Carol Belanger Grafton); *Old-Fashioned Illustrations of Books, Reading and Writing* (Carol Belanger Grafton); *Old-Fashioned Illustrations of Children* (Carol Belanger Grafton); *Old-Fashioned Nautical Illustrations* (Carol Belanger Grafton); *Old-Fashioned Romantic Cuts* (Carol Belanger Grafton); *Old-Fashioned Transportation Cuts* (Carol Belanger Grafton); *Perspective: Jan Vredeman de Vries* (Adolf K. Placzek); *Picture Book of Devils, Demons and Witchcraft* (Ernst and Johanna Lehner); *Picture Sourcebook for Collage and Decoupage* (Edmund V. Gillon, Jr.); *Trades and Occupations* (Carol Belanger Grafton); *Transportation* (Jim Harter); *Victorian Women's Fashion Cuts* (Carol Belanger Grafton); and *Women* (Jim Harter).

ACKNOWLEDGMENTS

The factual information contained in these stories was gathered from a variety of sources including *Atlas of Stars and Planets: A Beginner's Guide to the Universe* by Ian Ridpath (Facts on File, 1993); *The Book of Answers: The New York Public Library Telephone Reference Service's Most Unusual and Entertaining Questions* by Barbara Berliner with Melinda Corey and George Ochoa (Prentice-Hall, 1990); *The Compass in Your Nose and Other Astonishing Facts about Humans* by Marc McCutcheon (Los Angeles, Jeremy P. Tarcher, 1989); *Fodor's 96 Europe*, edited by Linda Cabasin (Fodor's Travel Publications, 1995); *The New Illustrated Universal Reference Book* (London, Odhams Press, 1933); *Perspective for Artists* by Rex Vicat Cole (Dover Publishing, 1976); *Planets and Satellites* (Barron's Educational Series, 1993); *Saints Preserve Us!* by Sean Kelly and Rosemary Rogers (Random House, 1993); and *Why Eve Doesn't Have an Adam's Apple: A Dictionary of Sex Differences* by Carol Ann Rinzler (Facts on File, 1996).

I would like to thank the Canada Council and the Ontario Arts Council for their generous financial support.

For their unwavering faith and their own special forms of devotion, I am deeply grateful to my friends Carla Douglas and Jim Kane (an extra thanks to Carla for the relish recipe on page 58), Merilyn Simonds and Wayne Grady, and Katherine Lakeman; to my agent, Bella Pomer; to Lois Rosenthal of *Story*; to my editors, Mindy Werner and Phyllis Bruce; and especially to Alex, my dear son.